THE BOY WHO KNEW DEMONS

BOOKS OF DARKNESS 1

BLAZE DZIKOWSKI

Editing by Lee at Ocean's Edge Editing

ISBN 978-83-942182-3-2

CONTENTS

— as told by the darkness

PROLOGUE

SOMEONE CALLED Gabriel's name that night.

Evening was falling over Los Maines, and the wind picked up, coming from the Pacific Ocean. It whistled among the sky-high cranes that still moved majestically above the industrial port. It blew over the dazzling skyscrapers of the business district, over the slum with the streets scattered with shit and used needles, over the lawns and swimming pools of affluent suburbs.

And a name was being heard on the evening wind, spoken and repeated by invisible mouths, louder and louder.

Gabriel.

Meanwhile, on the eleventh floor of a high-rise tenement in the heart of the city, a sixteen-year-old boy named Gabriel West was lying on his bed. His head hurt bad for the second week in a row. But he hadn't told his mother; she had enough worries as it was.

He had the window open to cool his tortured face.

And then Gabriel heard it. His name being called by a distant male voice outside.

"Gabriel!"

Grimacing from the pain in his temples, he crawled out of

bed and looked out the window. In the distance, the last sliver of the huge orange sun was setting low behind the office towers of the business district.

He looked at the neighboring housing blocks and he looked down at the yard. He couldn't see anybody calling him. But he thought he could hear his name still echoing in the canyons of the city: “el ... el ... el...” as real as anything else he heard.

He waited to see if the call would return, but the strange echo dissolved in the evening murmur of the streets.

He went back to bed. The headache receded a little; it seemed the pills had started to work. On the verge of sleep, just before he slipped into unconsciousness, he thought he could hear someone calling him by his name again.

And then he heard a million voices speaking at once, growing like the sound of the ocean, as if the city itself were talking to him, but he couldn't make out the words.

1

STRANGE PEOPLE

ON HIS TRUSTY Italian bike with paint chipped from years of use, Gabriel rode down the side street so fast his hair flew in the wind and his messenger bag with schoolbooks banged against his ribs.

This morning felt great, full of new hope. The air was cold and fresh. His two-week-long headache was gone and he toyed with the idea of finally gathering the courage to ask Andrea out.

Most of the kids at school were already seeing someone, or at least it seemed that way. A few days earlier he had read a piece online about how experts considered sixteen the proper age to start dating and he felt hopelessly behind schedule.

He passed by a dilapidated community playground with its rusty iron swings and sandbox full of dirty, gray sand. Surrounded by a chain-link fence, it had been closed for a long time, with a big padlock hanging from the gate, and Gabriel had never seen anybody playing there.

It spoke of short, unhappy childhoods, where a boy must quickly learn to fight and a girl quickly starts to put on makeup and pierces her ears. An inner-city playground. The old-time, metal swing-sets seemed too dangerous for the modern governance of the district. Afraid of a court case, and lacking funds for refurbishing, they preferred to lock it down.

Gabriel saw something. He frowned and slowed down. Some sick bastard had hung a pigeon on the fence. There was a noose made of wire wrapped around its neck and it hung there, stiff, dark and rotting.

"Gabriel!"

The voice was so close that he panicked, jerked the bike's handlebar and crashed to the ground. He got up on his knees and looked up at where the voice had come from. A sudden gust of wind hit the street, pushing apart old newspapers and empty soda cans.

In the deserted playground, behind the fence, a strange man was sitting on a swing and staring straight at him. The man was so pale that his skin was almost blue. His lips were thin and pale too, smiling a mean little smile. His bony face was specked with pockmarks, and his long, dirty hair was bound in a ponytail, sticking out from his mangy vagabond's hat. Over his black tracksuit he wore a dark, dirty coat. On his feet he had sports sneakers, grayed with time, raggedy and missing the laces.

But Gabriel paid attention only to his eyes, as they were the strangest thing about the man. The irises of his eyes were a fluctuating yellow color, like flames in slow motion.

The man jumped off the swings and spread his arms in a mock welcome.

"I was losing hope of ever meeting you. What with me being locked in this ... conundrum of a place."

Gabriel didn't answer.

The man laughed and came forward. "I see your parents taught you not to talk to strangers?"

Seeing as the man had no apparent way of reaching him through the fence, Gabriel gathered some courage, stood up and wiped his pants.

"Did you do that?" he asked, trying to sound manly and nodded at the pigeon. "That's abnormal, to say the least."

"Oh..." The man looked at the bird. "No, I haven't even noticed that, to be honest. Isn't it odd? You should feel pity for those weaker than you, and not aggression, unless you're very insecure and feel no control over your own life."

Gabriel shrugged and picked up his bike. It seemed undamaged.

"Anyway. So, now ... you're a Seer," said the man, and smiled even wider, revealing his gray teeth. "It was a long time coming. So many headaches since you were little. Nasty feeling, eh? Have your parents taken you to a neurologist? Waste of time and nerves, in my humble opinion."

Gabriel froze.

In fact, he hadn't told his mother about the headaches lately. He just kept stealing Ibuprofen from the medicine cupboard. The last time he told her about a strange headache, back when he was thirteen, she took him to a neurologist. They put him in a huge white tube at the clinic. Invisible rays penetrated his head and combed his brain with a deafening clatter. The neurologist couldn't find anything, and indeed it was a great waste of time, money, and his mother's nerves. But how did the strange man know all that?

Gabriel got on his bike. He was afraid again. His hands trembled.

"As you said yourself, I don't talk to strangers, that includes mental cases," he said.

"Now, you aren't leaving just when we finally met...?" said the man.

Gabriel shrugged and turned his bike.

"Wait ... please..." The man seemed genuinely sad to see Gabriel go. Gabriel's fear turned into anger.

"Get lost, weirdo!" he said and rode away.

The man still stood there behind the fence, watching Gabriel leave.

"See you later," the man called. "When you're ready! It's not like I'm going anywhere."

Gabriel had no intention of answering the hobo. He turned a corner and sped up, riding past a bustling marketplace. His hands were still shaking and his heart was thumping after the strange encounter.

WHEN HE ARRIVED at the school grounds, full of loud and cheerful students in colorful clothes, he calmed down a little. At Rosewater High, his daily problems became distant. Most of the time, Gabriel didn't feel understood by other kids at school. They never had it hard. Their problems were small and trivial: that someone had said something about them on the internet or they had gotten a grade that wouldn't satisfy their parents. They never feared about rent money, their parent's depression, new clothes for their quickly-growing little brother. But that was also why he could rest in their company and liked being there. He could feel like a teenage kid, one of them. And even though he was a bit timid, and he spoke little because he never could think of something clever or funny enough, the other boys seemed to like, or at least tolerate him. They were educated well enough to never show him disdain for being poor.

He decided that the man at the playground had been just a confused vagrant, nothing extraordinary in Los Maines. But how did he know about the headaches? And how did he know his name? Maybe he had seen him somewhere before...

As Gabriel put his bike in the school rack and walked to the building, he saw there were several strange adults on the school grounds. Adults weren't allowed in during class hours, so he was surprised to see a sad, obese woman sitting on the bench in the courtyard with a deflated basketball next to her. She didn't look like one of the teachers. There was something off about her. He thought she looked a bit like the crazy hobo from the playground: her skin was very pale, with a bluish hue.

In geography class, he sat next to his best friend Martin, an aspiring YouTuber, and behind Andrea, a girl he liked. Gabriel would love to ask her out, but didn't know how and he could never gather the courage, so he just sat and looked at her. Fortunately, he could do it for a long time in the classroom. Andrea lived with her father in the suburbs. She had curly, chestnut hair. When she peeked at her friend and laughed at a joke, her dark eyes turned almost golden in the sunlight falling through the windows. She was on the gymnastics team and had slim, tanned arms, which suddenly got covered with goose bumps and tiny, white hairs when a breeze came into class. She lifted her arm and then Gabriel saw the side of her breast and the black straps of her bra through the opening in her tank top and he let out a quiet sigh of wonder.

"What the ... where's that stupid thing?" said Ms. Carlyle, the geography teacher. She couldn't find a marker to draw the magnetic poles. After looking on the floor under the whiteboard and checking on her desk, she went to the back room. She came back with an old green marker in her hand. A thin, tall man in a green t-shirt followed her into the classroom. He stood silently next to Ms. Carlyle as she tried to draw with the dry marker.

Gabriel frowned. Who was the man from the back room?

"Eh, it's useless," she said and tossed the marker into a recycling bin in the corner. The strange man walked up to the basket and stood there, staring into it with a sad expression on his bluish face.

"Who's that?" Gabriel whispered to Martin, but his friend just stared at him, confused, then shrugged and returned to drawing stickmen in his notebook.

Gabriel thought the strange man from the back room was a mentally handicapped relative of the teacher and decided not to pay him any attention, just like Ms. Carlyle and the rest of the class. But he kept feeling something was off. He could feel a strange shiver in his chest.

As the bell rang and they were leaving the classroom, the strange man was still standing over the bin, staring at the discarded marker.

Gabriel met Andrea by the lockers. She smiled at him.

"Hi!" she said. "Are you okay? You look, I don't know, weirded out."

He smiled and nodded at her, grabbed his jacket and left in a hurry, leaving her wondering if she had said something wrong.

GABRIEL RODE HIS BIKE HOME, to the gray and crumbling high-rise, one of a dozen of identical buildings. He locked the bike in the stand, punched in the door code and entered the dark, depressing hall. He took the elevator to the eleventh floor, unlocked their apartment door, went inside and threw his bag in the corner, grabbed a cherry jam and peanut butter sandwich from the kitchen.

He entered his room and the sandwich fell out of his hand. An adult man with curly hair, dressed in purple overalls, was pushing himself into the corner with his face to the wall, and his shoulders were shaking as if he was crying.

Gabriel felt blood rushing to his head. He did not know what to do, his mind was completely empty. He looked around the room slowly and grabbed the first thing that could be used as a weapon: a small glass bottle of orange juice. Clenching the bottle tightly, he tried to sound confident and aggressive:

"What are you doing here?"

The man didn't react. It seemed as if he could not hear his words at all.

Gabriel couldn't take the pressure. He turned around and ran out of the apartment.

He shut the front door behind him, running down the stairs without even looking back to see if the man was following him. He was breathing hard when he ran outside into the yard.

Business in the yard was as usual. Old women with bags full of groceries were passing by; some kids played and yelled in the community fitness court, like colorful bats hanging upside-down from the rusty pull-up bars. Gabriel stood there paralyzed with fear.

Thoughts were racing in his head. Should he call his mom? No, she was working in the business district, cleaning offices. It would take ages before she came. He needed to be a man. He dialed 911.

"Nine-one-one, what's your emergency?" said a pleasant and calm female voice.

"There's—there's someone in our apartment," Gabriel said.

Staring at the entrance door, afraid that the man would come running at him, he told the woman about the stranger in his room. She told him to stay where he was, in a public space, and not to try going back to the apartment.

The police came faster than he expected. He heard a wail of the siren, saw the flashing blue and red lights, and the police cruiser pulled into the yard.

Two big guys in blue uniforms got out of the car. They took Gabriel's name and told him to calm down. He told them what happened. People were gathering around them. They wanted to know what was going on too. Finally, one cop reported something over his radio and they motioned Gabriel to come with them.

Gabriel rode in the elevator with the policemen in silence. He looked at a gun in one cop's holster. He shuddered as the elevator stopped at his floor.

He followed the cops down the hallway. They stopped at his apartment door. They gestured at him to stay outside. They took out their guns, opened the door and went in. Gabriel waited. His heart was pounding so hard his chest was shaking. It was silent. Finally, one of the policemen appeared in the door.

"Did you lock this door before you went outside?"

Gabriel shook his head. Why was the policeman so calm? Didn't they find the man?

"There's no one there. Must've run away. Come see if something's missing."

Gabriel nodded and went into the apartment.

"He was ... in my room."

"Go on, see if everything's in place."

Gabriel went into his room and screamed.

"He's here!"

The cops pushed past him and ran into the room.

"Where?"

Gabriel was pointing with his shaking finger at the man, who was still in the corner, still crying, with his back turned to the room.

"Can't you see him?"

He felt terror at the thought the policemen were in cahoots with the stranger and they would kill him together. Then he saw how the cops exchanged looks. And he understood.

"There's a man over there, in the corner!" cried Gabriel. "Can't you see him?"

"As a matter of fact, we can't see him, friend." The cop's voice was cold. "And as a matter of fact, do you realize there's a fine for pranks like that?"

"Come on, he's not pulling pranks," the other cop said. "The boy has problems."

"I'm not crazy!"

Gabriel tried hard not to cry. His eyes went back to the stranger in the corner. He was seeing him, as real as the policemen, as real as everything in the room. The older officer sighed.

"We need to take him to the station and run the tests."

"There's no one here," Gabriel said in a low voice.

The cops looked at him in surprise. Gabriel smiled at them.

"I'm sorry. Now I can see it was only a hallucination. I'm ... I'm not sleeping enough, and we have a lot of homework."

He looked hard at the cops. Were they going to believe him?

"I'm sorry for calling you without a good reason. Can we leave it at that, please?"

The meaner cop shook his head. "Look, pal, in that time we could be saving someone's life." The cop was stirring himself up and getting angry. "That's mighty irresponsible of you."

"Come on, man," said the older cop. "I'm hungry. The kid's learned his lesson."

MOM AND MATT were surprised to see Gabriel sitting on a bench outside.

"I just thought I could help you with those," Gabriel said, taking Mom's bags with groceries.

"Do you know what happened today?" yelled Matt, excited as ever. "Toby sank his Hot Wheels in the toilet!"

Upstairs, as they were taking off their shoes in the corridor, he peeked through the open door to his room. The stranger was there in the corner.

"Mom, come here, please," Gabriel said with difficulty.

"Yes?"

His mother came up to him and embraced him, kissed his head.

"Come with me," he said. "Matt, stay here."

"Why? I want to see too!"

"Matt."

Matt got offended and went to the living room.

Gabriel took a deep breath and led his mother into his room, waiting for her to gasp, for her cry of surprise. But she was just smiling at him, waiting for him to show her what he wanted.

“Look in that corner,” he said and pointed at the stranger, even though he already knew the result.

She did. Still smiling.

“What?”

“Nothing...” he said eventually.

Mom laughed, shrugged, and left the room. Gabriel picked up the sandwich from the floor, thought for a moment, and called Martin. He switched to video.

“Look what I’ve got here, man!” Martin said, shaking a bottle of beer in his hand. “Wanna come over?”

“No, wait. I’d like to show you something,” Gabriel said.

“Wow, are we going to cyber? If I knew I’d wear something sexier.”

“Look at that.” Gabriel ignored Martin’s attempt to be funny and pointed the camera at the man. At the same moment he realized it was all in vain, because on the screen there was nobody there. Just a wall. The phone didn’t see the man.

“Well?” Martin said, growing impatient.

“Call you later,” Gabriel said and disconnected.

He heard footsteps and turned to the door. He saw a child with a skull instead of its head. The little skeleton was standing in the corridor, staring at him with its hollow eye sockets and smiling with its bare teeth. Gabriel gasped; his heart skipped a beat, and then he realized it was just a Halloween mask. It was Matt in a mask.

“Play with me,” Matt said.

“Take it off!”

Matt slid the mask up over his head and stared at Gabriel.

“Play with me!”

“Tomorrow,” said Gabriel, thinking only about the strange man they couldn't see. “I’m tired.”

“And tomorrow you will say tomorrow. Please.”

Gabriel sighed. Finally, he asked: “What do you want to play?”

"Hide and seek! But you're searching!"

Matt loved hide and seek. He used to hide in the same place —the old closet in the hallway—so for the game to have any sense, Gabriel pretended he didn't know that. He would walk around the apartment and complain loudly that finding Matt was so difficult, and looked into the closet at last, finding a proud and triumphant Matt in there, and act surprised. But tonight he couldn't imagine doing that.

"No hide and seek. Lego."

They went to Matt's room and Gabriel lay on the carpet pretending to be interested in his brother building a space base and telling him what else should be in it. The kitchen. The bedroom. The toilet.

In the meantime, he was searching the internet for "hallucinations" on his phone. Possible causes included stress, anxiety, depression. True, he had been stressing out recently about the upcoming calculus test. He had to pass it with flying colors, because the Rosewater High stipend for "gifted children from marginalized parts of society" was the only thing that made his mom happy. She didn't want him to work, she wanted him to study. No wonder the test made him anxious. As he checked other search results, however, he couldn't rule out mental illness, such as schizophrenia or psychosis. And then he found a page about brain tumors and that did very little to comfort him further.

"You're not playing!" Matt said. "You're just staring at your phone!"

"Just a moment," Gabriel said. He stood up and went to the living room.

Their mother was half lying on the sofa in her faded, red bathrobe he remembered from his earliest childhood, watching the evening news on the TV. There was an interview with some government official about the Stellen Street Kidnapper. Six children had been missing for months, taken from various spots in Los Maines, and the cops still couldn't find a trace.

"Director Boleani," asked the agitated reporter, "it's been quite a while. How can you look those parents in the eye? You've found absolutely nothing."

"Ma'am, thank you for those questions," came the old man's answer. "You're obviously right. I'm very, very sorry that we haven't been able to identify the children's whereabouts. We've been working tirelessly, devoting days and nights, and the investigation is going well. I will not rest until this man is brought to justice and the children are back in the arms of their longing parents."

"Whew! Depressing stuff." Gabriel's mother shivered and turned off the sound. "You wanted something, cub?"

"Yeah, there's this strange thing. You know, Martin says he keeps seeing people who aren't there. Have you heard about something like that? Do you think there could be something wrong with him?"

His mother looked at him closely. "You're not taking drugs, are you?" she said.

"It's always the same!" Gabriel exclaimed. "You ask your parents anything and all they can think is you're a drug addict."

"I'm just worried that..."

"No, we're not taking drugs. Thanks for nothing," he said.

Truth be told, two months earlier they did try smoking some weed from the pipe that Martin had found in his brother's room. Gabriel did not like it. He couldn't get relaxed at all, he kept thinking about his childhood toys all the time and for some reason he fixated on his teeth and tongue, which seemed to him to be very big, forming a separate world of sorts. Yes, that was weird. But a couple of puffs could not cause a hallucination two months later. Could they?

"Let's make some dinner. Wanna help me?" she asked.

Gabriel spent the rest of the evening in silence, helping his mom cook dinner. They ate together with Matt and watched a show. Mom was saying how they would maybe get a streaming service if all went well with work. Gabriel replied it would be great. He tried not to think about the strange adult man crying in the corner of his room. He drank some of his mother's wine in the kitchen to relax. It was too dry.

But night was coming and he would have to go to sleep.

Trying to prolong the time before he had to go to bed, he spent good fifteen minutes in the shower. The hot water made him feel better and more sure of himself. He put on his sleeping trunks and t-shirt and went to his room. He looked at the man. The man was turned to the wall, covering his face with his hands, but Gabriel noticed the same blue hue on his skin, like the hobo from the playground and the strange adults at school.

"Goodnight, cub," called his mom from Matt's room.

"Goodnight," he answered. His voice sounded hollow. He couldn't tell her. He would end up either in an institution or a brain cancer ward. None of the options appealed to him.

"Who are you?" Gabriel whispered to the stranger.

No answer.

Gabriel hesitated, then reached up and switched off the lamp. The only light was coming from the neons on adjacent buildings. The man turned into a dark silhouette in the corner.

If the man were a hallucination, if he was only seeing things because of a brain tumor, there was nothing to be afraid of, was there?—apart from his impending death in a hospital. He lay down on his bed. What would happen to his mom and Matt if he died or went to an asylum?

Maybe in the morning the man would be gone, maybe Gabriel would heal himself in his sleep and become a normal, hallucination-free boy. He just had to fall asleep. Everything was alright.

Gabriel felt a sudden burning sensation in his eyes, and hot tears streamed down his face. He was crying in silence, afraid of the strange new world he was entering with no chance of return.

He didn't fall asleep. When he ran out of tears he just lay there, staring at the colorful shades the pulsating neons threw on his ceiling, and waited for the next day to come and set things right. From time to time he would rise on his elbow and throw a glance in the corner, but the man wasn't going anywhere.

After hours of this sleepless night, it started to get bright outside. And suddenly Gabriel remembered. He knew what he had to do.

He jumped off his bed, put on his dark gray hoodie to protect him from the morning cold. He wrote a note to his mother: *Just remembered I had to get to school early! See you in the afternoon. XXX.*

But school wasn't where he was planning to go.

2

DEMONS OF THE CITY

THE HALLWAYS of their building felt strange at this early hour. It was silent, save for some old tenant's cough coming through the walls, or a distant morning show on a radio with the monkey screams of the anchor, or hot water from morning showers humming in the pipes. It seemed several people were going to work much earlier than anyone else, or they just couldn't sleep.

Like Gabriel.

It was cold outside; the cool breeze hit his face and it felt much better than being locked up with the strange man in his bedroom. At least he was doing something. He unlocked his bike and rode quickly through the awakening city. An ambulance sped by, its siren's wail deafening in the morning silence. A group of trash collectors cleaning up a bus stop yelled something offensive at Gabriel, but he didn't listen.

When he arrived, he jumped off his bike, which fell to the ground with a clang, but Gabriel didn't pay any attention. His hair was dark and sticky with sweat under his hood. And there he was, the man from yesterday. The carousel spun around and the long-haired man with yellow eyes jumped out of it. He stood there, staring straight at Gabriel and smiling. The dead pigeon was gone.

"Who are you?" asked Gabriel. "Who are all of you? Those strangers at school, the man in my bedroom ... you. What is happening to me?"

The man kept silent for a while. "Well, you are seeing us."

"But who are you?" cried Gabriel in desperation.

The man stared at him for a while. And then he said it.

"We are demons, of course."

That's it, thought Gabriel. *I'm going crazy. Goodbye school, goodbye Mom, goodbye future.*

"You are not insane," said the man. "You can see us. You are the Seer. And soon you will become someone even bigger."

"You're dead?" Gabriel asked.

The man with yellow eyes smiled and shook his head.

"We are no ghosts of dead people. Demons, boy."

Gabriel waited for him to continue. He felt lightheaded and dizzy, about to faint. He grabbed the chain-link fence to keep himself from falling. The man came closer to the fence, inches away from Gabriel's face. Gabriel felt a strange, unpleasant smell, like burning plastic. Another ambulance sped by and the man began to speak loud in the noise of ambulance sirens and the awakening traffic.

"Everything in this world is alive, boy. Everything has its demon. Every living thing, and everything created by man has a soul borne out of its creator's intention. You want to know who I am? I am the demon of this forgotten playground. But you can call me Maurice."

"I can see demons...?"

"Christian demons. Native American Manitous. Jinns in Islam and Kami in Shintoism. Small gods. Spirits. We have many names. As we aren't the ones who speak them, we don't mind whatever you call us. We are ... like breaths of things, their secret life, the ... the embodiments of their essence. But how we look, how we appear to you, is just your imagination."

"But ... why am I seeing you now? Why did I become a, what did you call it? A Seer?"

"There are many mysteries in this world. It's one of them, I guess. I'm just a stupid demon of a playground, I don't have access to those great mysteries. I've heard there are people who can see us ... and I've met you, someone who can."

Gabriel laughed an unhappy laugh.

"You're crazy. No, sorry, you can't be crazy. You don't exist. I'm crazy."

The man's smile faded. He turned to the playground and yelled in a commanding voice:

"Come out!"

Gabriel watched in astonishment as the playground got crowded before his eyes. There was a curly-haired woman riding around and around on the carousel, laughing. There was a silly man jumping up and down beside a rocking horse. Another one hanging from the swings. A young woman sitting in the sandbox, rocking herself back and forth. They all had the same, pale blue skin.

"I am the demon of the sandbox!" the young woman yelled to Gabriel. "Small toddlers sit in me, they dig in me, build castles and dig tunnels. Where are they now? Why don't they come anymore?"

"I am Swings!" shouted the man hanging from the swings. "Up and down, fly to the sky, kick the clouds with your sneakers —so much laughter and exhilaration I give. But why is no one coming around anymore to swing, swing up and down?"

Gabriel looked at the man with yellow eyes who called himself Maurice.

"They talk like idiots," Gabriel said.

"Where are the children? Why are we alone?" yelled the demons.

Maurice turned to them. "Shut up!" he said. "Nobody's coming here because we're closed. It's over. No more kids."

The demons looked at Maurice, surprised, as if they didn't know him.

"And who are you? Yes, who are you?" they started to talk over each other.

Maurice turned to Gabriel and smiled.

"Completely demented. Please excuse us, we've been closed for so long."

He turned back to the demons "Shoo! Hide, the lot of you."

Complaining and lamenting, the demons melted into their homes and it was silent again.

"And the man in my room? What is he a demon of?"

"I have no idea. I don't know every demon in this city, that would be impossible. We are myriad. You'd have to ask him."

"I did, and he didn't answer."

"Because he couldn't hear you. You don't know how to speak to demons yet."

"I can talk to you," said Gabriel. "Is that any different?"

Maurice seemed confused for a fraction of a second.

"I'm a, uh, a bit special," he said. "I don't want to seem haughty, but truth be told I'm a bit brighter than most of that crowd. Next time you want to talk with a demon, just be confident. You can point at it and say: 'Listen!'"

Maurice cried the last word, pointing his thin and dirty finger at Gabriel, who didn't know what to say. There were so many questions, he didn't know where to start. So Maurice continued:

"When you want a demon to come out, just point at its totem and say: 'Come out!' Try it now."

"A totem?"

"Yeah. The thing which is our home. The thing a demon lives in. Anything. As I said, we are everywhere. And everything has a demon. Try it."

Gabriel pointed his finger at a trashcan on the other side of the street and said, without much conviction:

"Come out."

"Louder!" said Maurice. "It's a command!"

"Hey, you, in the trashcan! Come out!" yelled Gabriel.

And there appeared an old, shivering man, white-haired, shaking in an oversized, dirty jacket, with cigarette butts and crushed beer cans falling out of his pockets.

"Good!" Maurice said. "Now, talk to him."

Gabriel coughed. He couldn't think of anything to say. Finally, he forced out of himself:

"Hello...?"

The old man didn't seem to hear him at all. He whispered something to himself, shivered, and kept rubbing his shoulders.

"Now don't be such a softie," said Maurice. "You murmur. You need to have some conviction!"

"Okay..." Gabriel turned to the demon and pointed at him. "Listen!"

The old man stopped shivering and looked at him. Gabriel shuddered under the gaze of his pale, almost white eyes, with just black irises visible.

"Are you the Ombudsman?" asked the demon in a croaky voice.

Gabriel looked at Maurice.

"You're asking questions here," said Maurice dryly.

"Who are you?" Gabriel asked the demon.

"I am the demon of the trashcan and Kyle is my name. I am dirty and smelly and people of the city stuff me with impurities!" answered the demon. "They spit in me with green phlegm and throw spoiled food into my belly, and I am always, always hungry for more filth, young boy. Are you the Ombudsman?"

"Who is the...?" Gabriel asked Maurice.

"The Ombudsman?" Maurice chortled and said, "Oh, just a man who can talk to demons ... and command them to do what he wants. He can tell a car to stop, a padlock to open, a gun to never shoot a single shot anymore."

Gabriel listened to him in awe.

"And ... I'm an Ombudsman?"

Maurice looked closely into Gabriel's eyes.

"Do you want to be?"

Gabriel didn't answer. He wasn't sure what he wanted in this strange new world anymore. It was as if a whole unseen dimension had just opened before him. And he had no idea what do to with it yet.

Maurice coughed and looked down at his feet.

"I can teach you to command the demons," he said. "But I cannot do that when I'm trapped here in this smelly old playground. I want you to take me from here. Can you see the bulldozers down the street? My playground will be razed to the ground any day now and I will die. I need your help."

"What...?" Gabriel was stunned. Everything was happening so quickly.

Maurice stared at him with a serious expression, and as he continued speaking, there was a new, earnest tone in his voice.

"From the moment I was created, I dreamed of a different life. I want to do great things! I want to have adventures! Chase the bad guys, help the weak, be a force for good. I don't want to dic here, crushed by the bulldozers! If you take me from here, I can teach you how to command us. You are going to become the most powerful man in the city. And with my help, you are going to change the world. We will make a great team!"

"I want none of it," whispered Gabriel.

"Excuse me?"

"I don't want to see demons anymore."

Maurice was staring at him seriously, without a word. "Do you realize what kind of power I can give you?"

"I want to be a normal boy, like I was," said Gabriel. "I want everything to be normal again."

Maurice sighed. "It will never be the same again," he said

finally. "You cannot go back to who you were. But you can be the king of this city."

"I don't want to be a king. I want to be who I was."

"Gabriel," Maurice said. "Please help me. Take me from here. And I will make you very powerful."

Gabriel turned away from him, jumped on his bike and rode away. Maurice cursed under his breath.

As Gabriel was riding home, he felt the weight of the sleepless night. His eyes were closing. Sudden sleepiness filled every inch of his body. But he made it home before his family woke up. He destroyed the note he had left for his mother and sneaked back into his room, sat on his bed and pointed at the stranger crying in the corner.

"Listen!" Gabriel said. "Who are you?"

The man in the corner turned and looked at him with teary eyes.

"I am Music Player," said the sobbing man in a melodious, high voice.

Gabriel laughed. "What?"

The demon pointed at something under the heater and Gabriel had to stand up to check what was there. It was an old MP3 player he hadn't used for years once he got a better phone to listen to music on.

"The songs of joy, songs of longing, those sounds and words that took you to faraway lands and made you forget ... I gave you all that. There was a stream of beautiful feeling flowing through my headphones," said the demon.

"But, why are you outside your ... totem? Why did you come out?"

"Because the batteries are old and leaking and killing my circuits. I am dying, I am dying, Seer! And I need help."

The man raised his hands to Gabriel in a begging gesture.

"Please, help. If only in the gratitude for my tireless service. For all the songs I played to you when you were trying to fall asleep, sad and lonely in your bed at night."

"How can I help you?"

"Help me, oh, Seer! I beg you! I don't want to die."

Gabriel kneeled and took the dusty MP3 player from under the heater. Indeed, it didn't look well. There was rust around the hole where you put in the headphones.

"What am I supposed to do?" Gabriel asked. "I can't fix it. I don't even think there are any repair shops who do that anymore. It's an obsolete thing, an MP3 player."

The demon started to cry again.

"Look, I'm sorry. Please cheer up."

The demon cried even louder.

"I want to go to sleep! Would you be quiet?"

"Gabriel?" he heard his mother's voice from the corridor. "Who are you talking to?"

His mom was up already, and she heard him talking. The demon cried louder and louder. Mom opened the door and entered his room.

"You're dressed already?" she said, surprised.

Gabriel waited in anxiety—but no, she didn't see the demon, of course. Neither could she hear him.

"I couldn't sleep," he said, the demon's sobbing still drowning every sound in his ears. "I've dressed for school already. But now I think I shouldn't go."

"Why?"

"I'm feeling weak."

She put her hand on his forehead to check for fever.

"You look pale."

"Help me, I beg you, Seer," howled the demon behind him. It was hard to pretend he wasn't there.

"I feel like, my bones hurt, you know?" said Gabriel and rubbed his arm with a pained face. There was worry in his mother's tired eyes and Gabriel felt sorry he was lying to her. Her life wasn't easy as it was, without him suffering from insomnia and a mysterious bone sickness.

"It's not very serious, though," he explained. "Can I stay? I can feel tomorrow I will be good again. I just need to sleep."

"I will take Matt to the academy and take a free day at work too," she said.

"No! It's really unnecessary. Please, Mom. Go already. I just want to rest."

Mom hesitated for a second, then smiled and kissed him on the brow. She went out and closed the door behind her. Gabriel finally turned to the demon.

"Stop crying!"

"You're not an Ombudsman. You can't order me around," the demon answered through the tears.

Gabriel sighed. "Can I, like, talk to the demon of your battery?"

"Please do that, please."

"All right. Demon of the battery, come out!" said Gabriel.

Nothing.

"I guess I'd need to see it first," said Gabriel. He was so tired and didn't feel like looking for a screwdriver. "All right. I will deal with that later. Right now, can you let me sleep a little, please?"

"Of course. Sleep. While I'm dying."

Gabriel lay on his bed and pulled the comforter over his head. In the stuffy, warm darkness of his hideout he could still hear the demon's crying, but muffled and quiet. He fell asleep. At some point he must've moved the comforter off his head, however, because soon he heard another cry from the demon.

"Wake up! Please, Seer! Help!"

Helpless and angry, Gabriel jumped to his feet.

"I'm just a boy!" he screamed at the demon. "Stop it!"

He grabbed the MP3 player, opened the window and tossed

it out from the eleventh floor. The demon disappeared without a trace. The room was silent.

"Oh God, no." Now Gabriel didn't feel a slightest bit sleepy anymore. He opened the door and peeked into the corridor.

"Mom...?" he said carefully.

There was no answer. They had already left.

Gabriel put on his hoodie and went down to the yard. He walked around the building to the side his room was on. Eventually, he found the MP3 player. It was lying there on the sidewalk, smashed and broken. Good thing it didn't hit anyone on the head.

Gabriel kneeled over the player. He touched it with a tip of his finger.

"Hey, you ... are you okay?"

Nothing. Gabriel felt a terrible pang of guilt.

"Come out," he said.

Nothing. He'd killed the demon.

Back in his room, he threw himself on the bed in his clothes, closed his eyes, hid his head under the pillow, and fell into a long, dreamless sleep. In the sky above their high-rise, the clouds dispersed and beautiful sunlight turned the day into gold. That day, something very bad was going to happen.

3

TERROR

IT WAS A BEAUTIFUL, sunny day.

Gabriel's mother was waiting in line to the checkout at Rodder's Mall. She was worried about Gabriel. Little Matt was doing all right, as healthy and happy as a five-year-old should be. Now, Gabriel used to be a very easy child, too—always smiling, always playing. Until his father disappeared when she got pregnant with Matt. With each year Gabriel grew more quiet and self-conscious. He was timid and quiet among other boys. He just had one friend, that maverick YouTuber kid, Martin. He must miss his father, she thought.

Matt was a surprise child, eleven years after Gabriel. Her friends from work advised her to get rid of the pregnancy, especially as she was a single mom now, but she couldn't force herself to do it. Matt was the last thing his father left her.

The grandma in front of her paid and left and it was her turn. She started putting the groceries on the conveyor belt. The cashier smiled at her. He was much younger, but she could see a flirtatious spark in his eyes. That was inappropriate, but she smiled back. She believed a boy needs a man at home and she wanted to give her sons a new father. To be honest, that was the only reason she still wore makeup.

"Hello," the cashier said.

And then her mobile rang. She fished it out of her bag with one hand, still holding a carton of milk in the other, and frowned. The call was from Matt's preschool, Little Raindrop Academy.

"Hello...?" she said

The male voice in the receiver was fast and nervous.

"Ms. West? You've picked up Matt today, correct?"

Her legs felt weak, her heart skipped a beat.

"No!" she said, as anxiety crawled up her spine and grabbed her by the throat. The man didn't answer. There was silence.

"What happened?" she managed to say. "Where is Matt?" She held on to the counter not to fall as she cried into the phone one more time: "What happened?"

"We ... we will call you back in a moment," said the voice and cut the call.

"No! Wait!" she screamed.

The cashier and other customers were looking at her, sensing that something bad was going on. She dialed the number back. It wasn't answering.

She left her groceries on the counter and ran out of the store. She pushed through the people to the elevators. She banged on the call button. The elevator was so sluggish. She could hear her heart beating in her ears. She was afraid she would faint any moment.

As she ran across the underground garage, she crashed into a moving car. It hit her in the hip, but she just staggered. The driver stopped and yelled something at her as she continued running to her old Toyota.

She drove across the city as fast as she could, passing red lights, accompanied by screams of pedestrians she almost ran over and mad car horns, until she was at the Little Raindrop Academy. She stopped the car in front of the main gate, opened it with her card and ran straight in.

In the hall there were teachers and the security guard. They were staring at her, pale and silent, and in their eyes there was the unimaginable truth of what had happened.

"We can't find Matt," said the security guard.

"What do you mean?" she cried. "Nobody picked him up. You have to look for him! He must be hiding somewhere."

The principal stared at her and shook her head.

"We're waiting for the police," she said.

BEFORE THE POLICE ARRIVED, Joan forced the teachers to search the premises with her. Matt's things were still in the cloakroom: his shoe bag with a picture of colorful mouses, his NASA cap. They called for little Matthew to come out of hiding. They checked the classrooms, the halls, the bathrooms, the boiler room and the cellar. Outside they checked in the trees, in the tool shed, behind all corners, on all roofs. It was such a sunny, beautiful day.

And then the police arrived, along with somebody else. There were three regular police officers and there were two men, a very tall one in a jacket with an NBI logo and a basketball cap, and a shorter, black-haired man in a white shirt with a tie. The short man in the white shirt was ugly, with pockmarks on his face and black shiny hair sticking with sweat to his forehead, but he had the most intense gray eyes, burning deep in a bony face. He was cold and unpleasant, and the policemen were regarding him with obvious resentment.

The ugly man nodded at her.

"Ms. West? Senior Agent Andrew Delancey, National Bureau of Investigation. I will be in charge of the search." He nodded at the tall guy in the cap. "This is Agent Raymond Ayser."

. . .

THE NBI AGENTS told Joan to wait outside and took one of the classrooms as their base for questioning. They told everyone to stay out for the time being before they asked in witnesses.

"Sit down," Senior Agent Delancey said to his tall companion, pointing at tiny chairs and tables. Ayser smiled nervously. He wouldn't fit in any of them.

"Chill. In most cases, children are kidnapped or killed by family members," Delancey said, sitting on a table. "We don't know it's him."

"We wouldn't be here if you thought it wasn't him."

"Impressive powers of deduction. Come in!"

Someone was knocking at the door. It opened and a policeman brought in a little girl.

"I saw Matt," she said.

"What's your name?" Delancey asked.

"Ralia."

"Where did you see Matt, Ralia?"

"I was going to the nurse because I hurt my hand," Ralia said. "I saw Matt playing with his model car, and then he was playing with a ball. Then I saw him stand up, like someone was calling him. And he went to the back gate. But I didn't see him leave. I didn't see what happened later, because I went to the nurse."

"Did you see anything more?"

"I saw that there was somebody at the back gate waiting for him."

"What...?"

"There was a man."

Delancey looked at Ayser. "Then again, maybe it was him."

Ralia couldn't describe the man well. It was far away. She just saw he was wearing a green jacket and a baseball cap.

"A baseball cap! Like Agent Ayser?" Delancey pointed at Ayser.

Ralia nodded.

"But it wasn't him, was he?"

"No. The man was shorter and bigger. And his cap was red."

"Good, because otherwise we'd have to arrest Agent Ayser and put him in jail. Thank you, Ralia."

Delancey stood up. He really needed to go and give in to his secret habit. He gestured at Ayser and gave him a card.

"Give it to the boy's mother and send her home. Tell her to call me if she learns anything regarding her boy. There's still a chance his dad took him. Sometimes we get parental instincts at the oddest times. And for Christ's sake, tell her not to call me to just ask about progress."

DELANCEY LOCKED himself in the preschool bathroom. His hands were trembling again. He took a small syringe from the pocket of his coat and rolled up his sleeve. He found a vein and with a quick jab sent a dose of Atroposine up his veins. He gasped as he felt the electrifying wave flow into his body from this one point of injection. He could see how bony his arms had become. He was killing himself. But at least he could follow his only purpose without useless feelings and worries.

He smiled at a poster with a pink cartoon elephant, Cleanie, teaching children how to wash their hands.

"You're the boss, Cleanie," Delancey said.

Finding the Stellen Street Kidnapper was the sole reason he ate, walked, breathed. But it was the toughest case he had ever heard of. Half a year of futile investigation. Six children missing without a trace, taken from playgrounds, schools, their own home back yards.

Make it seven?

The case was eating Delancey inside. He felt helpless. Worthless. Angry and tired.

There was a knock on the door.

"Andrew?"

Delancey recognized Ayser's voice and opened the door. Ayser looked agitated.

"What is it?" asked Delancey, still reeling from the hit.

"We've checked the security recordings, as you told us."

"And?"

"The feed is erased."

"Brilliant."

THE PRESCHOOL JANITOR, an older guy who looked very obviously like an ex-police officer, seemed shocked with the entire ordeal. He was sitting there silently behind the narrow desk in his janitor room, the monitor of his computer throwing blue shades reflecting in his large rectangular glasses.

Delancey and Ayser stood above him.

"I didn't touch it," said the janitor. He was close to tears. "I swear."

The room was small and dark and filled with the smell of stale coffee and decades of janitor's lunches mixed with sweat.

"Show me," said Delancey.

The janitor turned to his computer and pressed the spacebar. Delancey leaned himself over his shoulder and looked at the screen.

The feed from the security camera showed the back gate. Timecode was 2:14 PM. A ball rolled by on the gravel path. Then Matt appeared. He ran following his ball and disappeared from view. And then, half a minute passed—and the view became all garbled, and turned to white static, like a TV set to an empty channel.

"It stays that way for over three minutes," said Ayser.

Delancey didn't answer. He was staring at the snowy screen. After three minutes passed, the image was back. The back gate was open, slowly closing, pulled by its the mechanical hinges. There was no trace of the boy.

"The camera must be broken," said the janitor.

"Just at the exact time the boy disappeared?" Delancey said. "How unfortunate."

The janitor lowered his head.

"Rewind it," said Delancey. "Let me watch it again."

The janitor rewound the recording and pressed play. Delancey leaned so close he could smell the irritating odor of the janitor's deodorant stinging his nose. The gate. The ball. The boy running after the ball.

"Pause!" Delancey cried.

The old janitor paused the recording. Ayser looked at Delancey in surprise.

"There," said Delancey and knocked on the screen with a tip of his fingernail.

In the upper left corner of the screen, on the other side of the fence, on the sidewalk, there was a pair of somebody's legs in old, black army boots.

Delancey reached over the janitor's arm and unpaused the video. It turned into static. Delancey pressed rewind and replayed the video at a slower pace. He grimaced as the janitor's hair tickled him on the side of his face.

"Could you?" he said and the janitor moved aside.

Delancey played the video at half speed. They watched as the unseen man's boots appeared in the corner and stopped next to the preschool's fence ... seconds before the feed went blank.

Delancey nodded at Ayser and they left the room.

"Do you think he erased the recording?" Ayser asked.

"He can barely operate this software."

"So ... what's the meaning of all this?"

Delancey stared at him with his piercing gray eyes.

"You tell me, ace."

. . .

Gabriel had slept for so long that he woke up dizzy. He moaned and sat on his bed and looked at the wall clock. It was 5:20 PM. The apartment was very quiet.

"Mom?" he called.

Gabriel stood up and walked through the apartment. Nobody. It was strange. At that time they were already home most days. Maybe Matt had managed to convince their mother to take him to a donut shop. Gabriel found his phone and called his mother. Nobody answered.

He went to the kitchen and made himself a hotdog in the microwave. The warm food tasted so good and reminded him he hadn't eaten in a long time. He was making himself a third one when he heard the signal from the intercom that meant somebody had just punched in their code and entered the building. Must be Mom and Matt.

The microwave dinged and Gabriel took out the hotdog in a warm bun. As he bit into the juicy, aromatic meat, he heard the apartment door being unlocked, and footsteps. There was something strange about the footsteps. He heard only his mom's. Usually there was a flurry of loud little footsteps and Matt would run into the hallway. And usually he talked a lot.

"Mom?" Gabriel said, putting the hotdog aside and going to the hallway.

His mother stood there motionless and stared at him like a frightened animal. Her face was wet with tears and black with flowing mascara. He looked at her in horror, his heart pounding in his chest.

"Matt is missing," she said finally.

"What ... what do you mean...?"

She walked up to him and embraced him and broke into tears. He was holding his crying mother and thoughts were racing in his head and none of them made any sense. Finally, she broke from the embrace and wiped her eyes.

"It's going to be all right," she said. "They're going to find him. The man from the police said that most children are found within twenty-four hours."

Gabriel nodded. "Maybe he just went somewhere on his own ... and got lost."

"Yes."

They both tried hard to not think of the words that immediately came to their minds. The Stellen Street Kidnapper.

"He was playing by the back gate," she said. "That's where they last saw him. Maybe he climbed over."

They were sitting in the kitchen in silence. Joan's phone was lying in the center of the table. They were staring at it. Joan connected it to the power so it wouldn't run out of battery. She would pick it up now and again to see if it was on and not in the silent mode. She put the paper card with Agent Delancey's contact information next to it.

The call never came.

Gabriel stood up. His mother looked at him, afraid. He took out his phone and snapped a photo of Delancey's card.

"I'm going outside," he said.

"No. Gabe ... please, let's not be alone now..."

"I can't be sitting here."

"But—not tonight!"

"Mom, I'm sixteen."

"Please, Gabe. I don't want to stay here on my own. Where are you going?"

"I'm going to look for Matt," Gabriel said.

4

THE SEER AND OMBUDSMAN

GABRIEL WENT to Matt's preschool. It was his former preschool too. He was standing outside the fence, staring at the flag floating on the mast. It was a windy afternoon, even though it was nice and bright, and the ropes rattled against the metal flagpole.

Gabriel walked along the fence until he came to the back gate. He saw the security camera on the wall. He pointed at it and said: "Come out."

A woman in uniform appeared. She had a very serious expression on her face and her hair was tightly tied behind her head.

"What is your need here?" she said. "What is your aim? I am a tool of the security here at The Little Raindrop Academy. It is my task to see everything, and every suspicious thing I see."

"I'm looking for my brother, Matt," Gabriel said. "He was last seen by this gate. Tell me what you saw."

"I will tell you nothing!" snapped the demon of the camera. "It is of no concern to you."

"I just told you my concern!" Gabriel replied angrily. "My brother is missing. Please help me."

"You are not authorized," said the demon.

Gabriel pointed at the gate. "Come out!" A strong, stern man appeared, his shoulders wide as a gorilla's.

"I am the Gate, the guardian of the little ones!" he said. "My job is to guard the safety of children and protect them from the bad world outside! Nobody can open me!"

"But you opened today," said Gabriel. "And my brother walked out through you."

The Gate didn't answer. He just stared into the ground.

"Well?" Gabriel pressed. "Who opened you today?"

"Go away!" the Gate cried. "I will not answer to you. For you might be a Seer, but I listen only to those who have the key."

"Please, how can I make you help me?"

"You cannot. My duty is my life."

"Hey, you!" Gabriel heard a voice.

It was the old janitor, walking towards the back gate from the preschool building.

"What are you doing here?"

"Nothing," Gabriel said, and he got on his bike and rode away.

THE PLAYGROUND WAS silent and empty.

"Hello?"

Silence. He extended his hand.

"Maurice! Come out!" he said.

He heard a laugh. And Maurice appeared right next to him, on the other side of the fence.

"I thought you wanted none of it," Maurice said. "And yet you keep coming here."

"My little brother is missing," said Gabriel.

Maurice grew serious. "I see," he said finally.

"I want you to show me how I can command the demons. I want to become the Ombudsman."

Maurice nodded slowly.

"We had a deal, though," he said. "You take me from here..."

"How can I do that?"

"I need a new container to live in, instead of this playground. Give me a new totem."

"Like ... what?"

"Whatever. Maybe... this thing on your wrist?"

Gabriel looked at the wrist of his right hand, where he wore an old, worn-out bracelet made of leather cord, a souvenir from their summer trip to Salvatore. He bought it at the beach. And he had forgotten about it long ago.

"Can I live in there?" Maurice asked.

"In my bracelet? I guess..."

"Also, there's ... one part of the deal I'm afraid we didn't discuss yet."

"What is it?"

Maurice sighed. "A small formality, really. I'm sorry I have to bother you with it. It's silly, to be honest. The totem has to be marked with something for me to enter."

"How do I do it?"

Maurice stared into Gabriel's eyes for a while.

"With blood," he said softly. "The fluid of life."

Gabriel took a shard of a broken bottle that was lying at his feet. He pressed it against the flesh under the thumb. He didn't even flinch as the glass cut his skin and a drop of blood appeared, cherry red, growing and growing in size.

He smeared the bracelet against the cut. His blood seeped into the leather.

"There," Gabriel said softly. "I have marked it."

Maurice opened his eyes, his mouth wide, and he started to scream.

Gabriel saw a demon come out of the bracelet—a demon of a blond, suntanned surfer in swimming trunks. Maurice was growing in front of the surfer, and the surfer cowered before him as Maurice screamed at him. His scream filled the air, and it lasted so long Gabriel thought he would go deaf. In the shrill scream, the bracelet on his hand became hot, so hot that Gabriel screamed, too.

And then it was silent.

The surfer was gone and Maurice was standing just next to him.

"You're ... in the bracelet now?"

"That's correct, Seer," said Maurice. "Thank you. I can finally leave this place."

"And ... that surfer? He was the demon of the bracelet before? Did you kill him...?" Gabriel felt guilty.

"You're such a little boy with a tender heart. Don't worry about it," said Maurice gently. "We are myriad. Thousands born and dead every minute. The wave of life, of new spiritual beings, is rising and falling in an endless ebb and surge. There's no place for crying over one demon."

"You're right," Gabriel said. "Help me find my little brother."

"How about we find some more intimate place," Maurice said. "I'm afraid we have company."

A homeless man, wrapped in several winter jackets and woolen caps, was staring at Gabriel suspiciously from the corner.

"You're correct," Gabriel said. "Where do you want to go?"

Maurice smiled. "Your choice, Seer. I know only my playground."

Maurice disappeared, but the small vibration and a touch of heat from the bracelet told Gabriel that Maurice was now hidden in it.

Gabriel got on his bike and rode away.

"You should seek professional help!" the homeless man yelled after him. "Those voices aren't real, you know?"

. . .

HE COULDN'T GO HOME, his mother would hear him talking to the invisible demon. He needed to find a place where they would be alone and could talk freely.

So he rode to the port. He sat on the concrete embankment over the dark waves. Distant phantoms of transoceanic freighters loomed on the horizon. On his right, far away, was the bridge to Calatoo Island, cars and trains going over water.

He looked at the leather bracelet.

"Come out," he said.

Maurice appeared next to him and looked around.

"No. No, no, no, no..." he murmured.

"What's wrong?" Gabriel asked.

"I ... really don't like big water," Maurice hissed and disappeared back into the bracelet.

"Oh come on!" Gabriel cried in exasperation, but there was no answer.

He got back on his bike and looked around. Where would they be left in peace? He had another idea. He rode back home. On his way, his mother called him. Gabriel said everything was all right and asked if the police had called her. They had not.

Gabriel unlocked the door to his apartment building with his key. He didn't want to use the intercom, or his mother would know that he was back. He took the elevator to the top floor. There was a long corridor stretching all across the width of the building. At the end there was a ladder and an iron door to the roof, locked with a padlock he knew was broken.

A flock of pigeons fled in panic when he climbed to the roof. As he stood there, the wind was blowing in his face. Seagulls were circling above him, crying in their plaintive, strangely human-like voices. The dusk was falling. He could see the first lights appearing in windows of the other apartment buildings in his neighborhood. In the distance, he could see the trees and parks of the affluent suburbs, and further still two very high, black towers, with red blinking lights on their tops. In another direction, he could see the skyscrapers of the business district, industrial machinery of the cargo port, and the ocean.

"Well?" he said. "Come out."

Maurice appeared next to him.

"Ahhh, much nicer," he said, and sat on the edge of the roof, his feet in dirty sneakers dangling over the street below.

"What was that about the ocean?" Gabriel asked.

"Yeah, I don't know, really. Maybe I'm a tad agoraphobic."

"What?"

"Afraid of big, open spaces ... or maybe I just don't like water."

"Is this good place?" Gabriel asked.

"It's perfect," Maurice said.

"Well?"

Maurice sighed. "You must know that there was ... a pact between humans and their creations," Maurice said, staring into the distance. "The Covenant. And there is a secret Sign of the Covenant that forces all demons of things to listen to a man who shows them the Sign."

"Even you?"

"Even me?" Maurice laughed. "You think I'm so powerful? Yes, even me ... but, is there any reason to order around a demon of some old playground?"

Gabriel shrugged. "And you know that sign, yes?" he asked.

"I happen to know it, that's right."

"How do you know it? Where from?"

Maurice got befuddled. "I have to be honest with you," he said. "I don't know. I just knew it since the time I was created. Maybe it's a gift, maybe it's a mistake ... maybe destiny, if anything like destiny exists. I just know the Sign."

"If it helps me find Matt, I'm fine with everything..."

"One more thing, before we begin."

"Yes?"

"Whatever happens, don't tell the adults, and especially the police or military. They will lock you up so they can have your power."

"Teach me this sign," Gabriel said.

Maurice jumped to his feet and Gabriel gasped, sure that the demon would fall off the roof. But nothing like that happened.

"Left hand," Maurice said. "It only works with the left hand. Extend your fingers. Now, curl your forefinger. And move your hand as if you were writing an inverted capital 'D.'"

Maurice put his hand to his chest, bent his forefinger and moved his hand in half-a-circle. Gabriel repeated the gesture.

"That's it?" he asked.

"That's it ... Ombudsman," Maurice answered.

Gabriel looked at him and took a deep breath.

"And you have to listen to me? I can tell you whatever I want and you must obey me?"

"I can't do things I can't do," Maurice explained. "If I told you to fly off this roof you couldn't do that even if you wanted to, because humans don't fly."

"Okay."

"And as I am just a piece of string around your wrist, my powers are limited to say the least. I can't even tighten or loosen up, because the knot doesn't permit that. I could maybe untie the string ... and fall from your hand ... and that would be the full extent of what I can do at the moment. But you'd be hard-pressed to find a better advisor. I've existed since 1976. In that time I've heard many things from mothers and fathers. Parents get bored on a playground and like to talk with each other while guarding their kids. And I had nothing better to do than listen."

"Okay, okay, stop talking."

Gabriel looked around. His gaze stopped on a ventilation shaft. A huge fan was turning in the metal case, slicing the air.

"Come out," Gabriel said.

A big, fat man appeared next to the ventilator. His face was covered with machine oil.

"Round and round I go," said the demon. "So the air moves in the shafts, so I pump life-giving air to humans, who live here."

Gabriel stood before him and made the Sign with his left hand.

"This is the Sign of the Covenant," Gabriel said.

The demon of the fan looked at Gabriel, squinting his eyes, and nodded.

"So it is," he said with impatience. "And...?"

"Stop the fan," Gabriel said.

The big fan went slower and slower until it stopped.

Gabriel felt his heart beating stronger.

"Now, move it faster," he ordered the demon.

The fan moved and gained speed.

"Faster!" Gabriel cried. "Go faster!"

He watched in elation as the fan gained speed and became so fast its blades turned into a blur.

"Please!" yelled the demon. "Please!"

"What is it?" Gabriel shouted over the noise of the rotor.

"I'm breaking!" cried the demon.

Smoke was coming out of the mechanism and Gabriel smelled the burning insulation. But he couldn't stop looking at it. He was the most powerful man in the world. The possibilities of what he could do were dizzying.

"I beg you!" the demon cried.

"Okay, you can stop!" he told the demon.

Gabriel turned to Maurice, who had been observing the show with amused interest.

"Now we go find my brother," Gabriel said.

5

THE MAN IN A MASK

BACK ON THE STREET, Gabriel invoked the demon of his bike. It was a tall, energetic young man in Lycra. His name was Giovanni.

"I am your demon of speed!" Giovanni exclaimed. "Faithfully taking you from one end of the city to another! And I never tire! Let's go!"

Gabriel jumped on his bike. It was getting dark. He dashed down the road, under streetlights, a Mickey Mouse charm dangling from the handlebar. Maurice moved through the air beside him, smooth and cool.

They stopped by the preschool back gate. Gabriel invoked the demon of the security camera.

"You again!" the woman said with anger. "I told you not to bother us when we perform our solemn duties of security! Go away!"

"I will not go away," Gabriel answered, and made the Sign of the Covenant. "I am the Ombudsman."

The woman shivered and stared at him, surprised. Gabriel continued:

"A young boy, my little brother Matthew West, left through this gate today. Did you see him? Did you see how it happened?"

The woman went quiet. She hung her head low and stared at the gravel path under her feet.

"Well?" Gabriel said. "Have you?"

"I see everything that happens here..." the demon of the camera said in a quiet voice.

"Well? How did it happen?"

The woman finally stared at Gabriel.

"But this, I didn't see," she said.

"What?"

"I have seen your brother, I know Matt well. The last I saw of him, he was running after his ball, the one he likes to play with so much. And then ... I had to stop looking."

"What? You're lying!" cried Gabriel.

"Ombudsman..." It was the calm, quiet voice of Maurice. Gabriel looked at him. "They can't lie to you. You are the Ombudsman."

Gabriel turned back to the demon.

"Why did you stop looking?" he asked the Camera.

"Looking is my duty and my being. What I see, I see. But I was told to stop looking and I had to obey."

Gabriel and Maurice stared at each other.

"Who told you to stop looking?" Gabriel asked.

"A man I had to listen to."

Gabriel stared in horror at the demon of the camera.

"What man?"

The Camera turned her head away and didn't say anything more.

"Come out!" Gabriel cried with desperation to the gate.

The strong guard appeared.

"Again? What do you want? Beat it!"

Gabriel made the Sign and the demon shut up.

"Yesterday, a little boy went through you even though your duty is to remain locked all the time, like you said earlier."

"Yes, Ombudsman."

"How? Did he unlock you somehow?"

"No. There's not a child in the whole Little Raindrop Academy that can open me. Because I am their protection."

"What happened, Gate? How did Matt get outside? Why were you unlocked?"

The demon of the gate clenched his jaw; his face grew dark, and staring hard at Gabriel he hissed:

"Because a man came by and ordered me to unlock."

"Who was he?"

"He was a man who knew the Sign and who knew the Covenant. And I had to listen. And he told the camera to stop looking. He grabbed your brother by the hand and he took him. He took him!"

"He knew the Sign...?" Gabriel whispered. "Another Ombudsman?"

He turned to Maurice. "Didn't you tell me I was the only one in this city?"

Maurice didn't answer.

"Describe him to me," Gabriel ordered the demon.

And suddenly other demons started appearing, ready to give their accounts of what they witnessed. They jumped out of the fire hydrant, out of the sidewalk, out of a bench. Gabriel turned from one excited demon to the next, taking note of their words:

"Big, bulky man ... formed like a big child ... heavy, dirty boots on his feet, army boots ... dark-green military jacket. And he had black hair, cut very short. But his face was covered with a mask!"

"Wait, don't speak all at once! A mask? What mask?"

"Blank. White mask. Blank mask. With just holes for his eyes," said the Gate.

"So, what did, what did Matt do when he saw him?" Gabriel asked the Gate.

"The man said: *Hey, pal!* Those were his words. I remember well."

"Yes! *Hey, pal!*" the other demons attested.

"And your brother looked at him and smiled and said *Hey*," the Gate went on.

"He smiled at a strange man in a mask? That's bullshit!" Gabriel said.

"That's what happened! Exactly!" the other demons said.

"And then?" Gabriel asked.

"And the man said, *Come here!* As he was saying it, I was open already," said the Gate. "And your brother came to the man ... and the man held out his hand, a strong hand, strong hand with dirt under his fingernails ... and Matt took it. Matt took the man's hand. And the man led him away."

"That's impossible! Matt would never go with a man he didn't know!"

"But he knew him," said the Hydrant.

"What!"

"Your little brother knew the man, I'm positive of that. There was a smile on his face. There was confidence in his gait."

Gabriel didn't know what to say. Finally, he managed:

"Did he say anything to the man?"

"He said something strange."

"What was it?"

"He asked: *Why are you dressed like that?*"

There was silence.

"Did the man answer him?"

"No."

"Where did the man take him?"

"He took Matt to a white van. A van as white and blank as his mask. He said, *Get in, buddy. Where are we going?* asked the little boy. *Somewhere fun*, answered the man, *we are going to have fun.* And Matt laughed, and his laugh was very happy."

Gabriel clenched his jaw.

"Did you see the license plate?"

"I didn't," said the hydrant.

Gabriel turned to the demon of the sidewalk.

"You are low above the ground! Did you see the license plate?"

The Sidewalk was a quiet, frightened weakling, dressed in gray coveralls.

"I, I guess I did, but ... but..." he stuttered.

"But what?!"

"I just didn't pay attention to it. I am sorry ... I thought it was just another car."

"Are you joking?" Gabriel cried.

"Ombudsman," Maurice said quietly.

"What?"

"We are not all-knowing. We are just your handicapped creations. You can't expect too much from us."

Gabriel kept silent for a while, then he nodded and turned to the Sidewalk.

"Where did the van go?"

Nobody answered.

Gabriel looked at the street and pointed at it.

"Street. Come out."

The demon of the Street was a fast young girl, dressed in leather. She was smiling manically and shivering with energy.

"I am a city street!" she cried. "A man-made way, bustling with speed and motion. What do you want of me, Seer?"

"I am an Ombudsman," Gabriel told her. "Today, a white van took my brother from here. Where did it go?"

"A van?" the Street asked.

"A white van, driven by a man in a green jacket, with a white mask on his face. I command you, tell me where it went."

The girl laughed. "Thousands of cars crash my surface, thousands of cars I carry to their destinations. It is a foolish expectation that I could remember each and every one of them, their starting points and finish lines."

Gabriel turned to Maurice. "Is she doing this on purpose?"

Maurice shrugged.

"You are the Ombudsman. We have to listen. But there are many limits to our minds."

Gabriel tried one more time:

"Please, think," he said to the Street. "Just a general direction?"

"I am one way, don't you see?" the Street chortled. "Unless the driver broke the law ... but he didn't, as I would have remembered such an occurrence."

"Would you know where he turned? You stretch from here, up to, I don't know..."

"Up to the Constitution Square," the Street answered. "And along the way I intersect, I intersect! With 23rd and 22nd and 21st Avenue, you know? And I finish my run in the arms of Constitution Square."

"I can go and ask the square," Gabriel said.

"I can do that for you. I'm there already," the Street said. "I am here and I am there, and I am down at the suburbs where I start my run,"

"Please ask the Square."

The Street closed her eyes and was silent for a second. Gabriel waited. She finally opened her eyes and looked at him with sympathy.

"While there are hundreds of cars on me every hour, there are thousands of them on the Square. He is old and tired and says everyday tens of white vans circle his dominion. I am sorry, Ombudsman."

"That's okay. Thank you."

Gabriel thought for a while, then turned to Maurice.

"Okay. Let's go."

"Where are we going, Ombudsman?"

"To the police, to tell them what we know. A man in a white mask, whom Matt seemed to know, put him in a white van and drove toward the Constitution Square."

"I have just one question," Maurice said.

"Well?"

Maurice put on a voice, pretending to be a policeman on duty.

"*How do you know all that, buddy? Did you see the man? Did you see the van?*"

Gabriel knew what Maurice was hinting at.

"I heard it from the demons," he said with a sigh. "The police won't believe me."

"They might think you're a basket short of a picnic," Maurice agreed.

Gabriel sat on a bench and took his phone out of his pocket. He opened the browser app and created a new email account. Name? *The Ombudsman*. Age—*100 years old*. Then he found the photo of Agent Delancey's card and copied his email address. And he wrote him an email, in which he described everything he'd learned from the demons in the back yard of the Little Raindrop Academy.

"Interesting," Delancey said, staring at his phone. He was reclining in his swivel chair in the bullpen of his department, with his legs resting on the top of his desk. "Bea?"

Beatrice, the second agent in his team, a tall, black-haired woman, had just come in. She was still in her leather jacket. She walked up to his desk and asked him what he wanted.

"I got an email from an anonymous source. *Matt West, the boy who went missing today, possibly knew his kidnapper. The man was dressed in a green jacket and black army boots. He opened the back gate, took Matt by the hand and led him to a white van. They drove off towards Constitution Square.*"

They looked at each other.

"Who sent it?" Beatrice asked.

"Someone calling themselves the Ombudsman. I've already

run a search, but it's nowhere on the net. Appears it's fresh. I will forward the email to the IT guys to run an analysis on it."

"You think there's something to it?"

But Delancey was already on his phone, ordering the traffic division to check all recordings for a white van at the time of the disappearance.

"We get loads of unsubstantiated tips from the people," Beatrice said. "How do you know this one's worthwhile?"

"One, because the disappearance wasn't yet reported to the public. Two, because they have the boots right. Now I have a question."

"Shoot."

Delancey took a glance at an old-fashioned watch on his wrist.

"Can we go to my place after work tonight?" he asked. "To let off some steam?"

"You're a hopeless romantic, Senior Agent Delancey," Beatrice said. She leaned over him. "It's my husband's birthday," she whispered in his ear.

"Oh, okay. Give him my best wishes."

"Of course I will. And now I need to fill in my reports."

Beatrice left the office. Delancey watched her walk into the elevator.

They had been sleeping with each other for over three years. One, two times a month. They did it for the first time after the baby shower Ayser threw for his newborn girl. On their way back from Ayser's home, they touched each other and kissed in the back seat of a cab, and took a detour to his apartment.

Delancey knew Beatrice loved her husband, and if she had to choose she would stop sleeping with him in an instant. Sometimes he wondered whether she had problems with her conscience. But Beatrice was the most down-to-earth person he'd ever known. She liked sleeping with him, she liked her husband, and she appeared to see no problems with that. She didn't think she was hurting her husband, because he didn't know about anything, so how could he be hurt? It all made sense, but Delancey still admired her unwavering sensibility. It was almost inhuman. That's why he liked it.

And he hoped it would save her life one day.

6

FACES

When Gabriel returned home and his mom came out to greet him, he noticed she held a small cross on a chain in her palm. They'd never brought up religion in the family before. She said she'd been to the local church and prayed for Matt to be found. She asked Gabriel if he wanted to go with her next time. He said he'd think about that.

He went into his room. Maurice sat on his bed.

"It's better we don't talk too much," he said. "Your mama can't hear me, but she hears you all right. I bet she has enough worries as it is."

"I don't feel good sitting here and waiting," said Gabriel. "I'm not tired at all. I can't sit in one place. Remember what you told me at the playground? That you dreamed of adventure, chasing bad guys, helping the weak? And now you want to sit here?"

"Sometimes rest is the best. And unless you want to go to church like your mother, there's not much else we can do now," Maurice said.

Gabriel ate dinner with his mother. In silence, they watched the news about Matt missing on Los Maines' local TV channel. As the reporter said that questions were arising whether the case was connected to the Stellen Street Kidnapper, his mother immediately changed the channel.

They watched a documentary about the growing use of drones in many areas of life, in surveillance, transport, even crime. "It is hard to underestimate the impact drone technology will have in the years to come," the narrator said.

Joan's phone rang, and she tried to answer it so fast it fell out of her hands and the screen cracked. It was one of Delancey's agents calling, a woman named Beatrice. She said there was nothing new to report, but they should remain strong. Gabriel's mother nodded and said she understood.

Later, Mom told Gabriel that he had to go to school tomorrow and carry on. She embraced him and promised him everything would be alright. He could feel her body trembling, and saw the dark rings under her eyes. She took some sleeping pills after dinner, and he watched her eyes closing.

She fell asleep on the sofa in the living room. Gabriel turned off the documentary about drones, covered her with a blanket, and switched off the light.

He pointed at the sofa.

"Come out," he whispered.

The demon of the sofa was a good-natured chubby man in an old, baggy sweatsuit. He nodded with concern when Gabriel commanded him to keep his mother warm and comfortable that night.

Then Gabriel paid a visit to Matt's room. It was heart-breaking how silent it was. Matt always made so much noise. Now the bed was empty and cold, the toys strewn over the floor where he had left them in the morning, when he had been trying to get in some fun with his action figures before it was time to leave for preschool.

Gabriel stood there in silence and felt tears welling in his eyes. He shook his head and chased them away. He had promised himself to be tough. He refused to mourn until there was no hope. He looked in the corner of the room and jerked in fright when he saw a dark figure by the window. Only then he realized it was the demon of Mr. Banks, the Lego figure Matt built out of parts from different sets and played with him the most.

Mr. Banks turned his worried face to Gabriel.

"Where is Matt?" he asked quietly.

Gabriel didn't answer.

"Where is Matt?" asked the demon of Matt's racecar, an agile sportsman in checkered coveralls. "Where's our Matt?" asked the soldier in a fluorescent orange uniform, the demon of Matt's NERF gun.

Gabriel didn't answer the quiet choir of questioning toys.

He closed the door behind him.

Gabriel told Maurice it was time to go to sleep. He lay on his bed and stared at the ceiling. The lights on the ceiling moved as neons colored the walls of his room. He listened to the distant hum of the city night.

Somewhere out there was Matt, frightened and waiting for help.

In darkness, Gabriel got off his bed and put on his hoodie.

He told the demon of the front door to be very quiet when he unlocked it. He didn't want to wake his mother.

He wandered the night streets, calling out the demons of the lampposts, bus stops, hydrants, the demons of the streets and sidewalks. He kept asking them the same question: *Have you seen my little brother? Have you seen Matt?*

Beatrice yawned and stretched in her chair.

"It's eleven. Time to call it a day," she said to Delancey. "Aren't you going, boss?"

"Just a second. You go, Bea."

She looked at him with worry. She had never seen him so consumed with his work before.

"Hey," Delancey said, "look at that."

He had an email from the traffic division. They'd managed to find a white van in the security footage one block away from Matt's preschool. Delancey opened the image attached to the email and he froze. There it was. A white van in traffic. The driver was not very clear, but Delancey saw a man in a white mask.

"What is it?" Beatrice asked.

"Come here, please," Delancey said. "Take a look at this."

Beatrice leaned over him and looked at the screen.

"It's George!" she exclaimed. "What is this photo?"

"What?" asked Delancey with disbelief.

Beatrice seemed dumbfounded.

"Well ... it's my George, no? Behind the wheel. Is that ... some kind of a joke? What is this van?"

"Your husband? How do you know it's him?"

"What do you mean? I can see his face."

Delancey looked at the image again. "It's a man in a mask," he said.

"A mask of George? What's ... Andrew, what's this about?"

Delancey closed the image and stood up. He began pacing to and fro. Beatrice looked at him in fear.

"Andrew, could you please tell me what is the meaning of this? Why do you have a photo of George in that car?"

Delancey forced a laugh. "Well, we ... we're trying a deep fake technique. They photoshopped your husband into the photo."

"Well, I'm not sure if I like that. Why would you do that?"

"I'm sorry, Bea. I didn't think it would upset you like that. It was just a test of their new software."

"Well, I got anxious, because you looked as if you saw a

ghost. You made a very strange deal out of that if it's supposed to be just a test."

"I'm sorry. I just didn't know they could do that so well. Thank you, Bea. I'm going to delete that."

Beatrice kept silent for a while. Finally, she spoke.

"I, I think ... Andrew, you should take a rest, as well. You are starting to behave strange."

"I will. I'm sorry. Good night, Beatrice."

After a while, she nodded and left the room.

Delancey quickly went back to the computer and opened the image again. It was not Beatrice's husband he was seeing behind the wheel of the white van. It was an unknown man with his face covered by a featureless, white mask. Why was she seeing her husband?

The door opened and in came Ayser, already in his bomber jacket. His basketball cap's beak was pointing straight at the ceiling. You could always tell what humor Ayser was in from the way he wore his cap: from the beak straight up when he was happy to leaning on his nose and covering his eyes when he was blue.

"I can drive you home," Ayser said, and then he saw Delancey's changed face. "What is it?"

Delancey was thinking on his feet. His throat felt dry. He made a decision and moved away from the screen and uncovered it.

"I got an image from the traffic division. They found this image of the white van by the preschool. Given the number of white vans in the city, it's a stretch, but the image is interesting."

"Do you have a license plate?

"Nope. But the driver is visible."

"Wow! If your informer's legit, that could be a major—"

Ayser walked up to Delancey's desk and looked at the screen. Delancey watched for his reaction. Ayser frowned, then shook his head and looked at Delancey, then back to the screen.

"I ... I don't understand," he said finally. "Are you making fun of me?

"Who do you see?"

"Well, why do you ask me that? What do you mean, showing me that?"

"Who do you see?!" asked Delancey.

"Isn't it you? I see you."

"You're seeing me?" Delancey said softly. "Driving that van? In the photo?"

Ayser glanced at the screen once again.

"I ... isn't that you...?"

"Beatrice saw her husband driving that van," Delancey said. "I'm seeing a man in a mask. Are you seeing me?" He laughed. "It's ridiculous."

"Andrew, are you playing with me?"

"I am not playing with you, Ray."

He looked through a glass window separating the bullpen from a corridor and saw a familiar silhouette.

"Let's call Benny."

"Why do you want to call him?"

"To see what he sees. Benny!"

The door opened and Benny, the jovial, pudgy cleaner, peeked in.

"Good evening..." Benny said with hesitation.

"Good evening, Benny. We wanted to ask you for help."

"I'm gonna clean your office in an hour, after I do the hall..."

"No, it's not about cleaning. Please take a look at something and tell us what you think."

"Uh. Okay..."

Benny put his mop aside and trudged toward them.

"Look at the screen, Benny. Who do you see in that van?"

Benny squinted and moved his head closer to the screen.

"Wow! Oh my," he said. "It's Meg!"

He moved away from the screen and looked at the agents in surprise.

“Meg?” Delancey asked.

“Why, my daughter! What is she ... how do you ... is that her car?” Benny was growing anxious. “Is she in trouble?”

Delancey and Ayser exchanged looks.

“She’s not in trouble,” Delancey said. “We’re just ... testing a new application. That’s not your Meg, just someone who’s very similar.”

“Uh ... okay...”

“Someone who looks like many different people, apparently,” Delancey said, looking at Ayser.

“Wow. I could swear it was my girl, Agent.”

“That would be all. Thank you, Benny.”

When Benny left, Delancey dropped to his chair and covered his eyes.

“How do you explain this?” he gestured at the screen.

“Well...” Ayser examined the screen. “The image is not very sharp. It’s dark. We are tired. I gather, maybe our brains fill in for the details that are missing from the photo, and we fill that in ... with people we know.”

Delancey was looking at Ayser in silence. Finally, he nodded. “I’m going to accept that.”

“Yes?”

Delancey chortled without much humor. “What other choice we have?”

“Aren’t there more images from the traffic?”

“Several. But none with the face or the plates.” Delancey shook his head and sighed. “There’s always been something weird about that case,” he said, rubbing his tired eyes. “Some days I’m afraid I’m losing it, Ray.”

“You just need to rest,” Ayser said.

“Wait. I have an idea. Let me put it through the face recognition software.”

He opened an app on his laptop and moved the image file into it and ran the scan. They didn't have to wait long for the result.

NO FACE FOUND

Ayser laughed. "It's ridiculous."

"Okay. Let's say it's inconclusive," Delancey sighed and closed his laptop. "Excuse me."

He felt his pocket. Yes, the familiar shape of the mini syringe. He went to the bathroom. He quickly rolled up his sleeve and found the vein. At the same split second when the needle pierced his skin and entered the vein, he heard Ayser slamming at the door.

"Chief! We have a body."

7

DEAD CHILD / CARNIVORE

THE MISERY LIGHTS on the roofs of police cruisers threw shades of blue and red on sky-high piles of waste. Delancey and Ayser followed an officer from the night patrol as they navigated the heaps of trash. It stank like shit, and Delancey, who had his senses heightened by Atroposine, found it hard not to vomit. The stars shining above the dump on the outskirts of the city looked like white shards of diamond against the purple, artificial aurora from the urban light pollution.

In the sickly light of a bare bulb, the night watchman standing by his guardhouse seemed drunk and frightened. Two uniformed officers were interrogating him. They nodded as they saw Delancey.

"Agent," one of them said.

"I didn't do nothing! As I saw it, I called you at once!" wailed the watchman, staring at Delancey with pleading eyes. "Please, can I have my mints? I have them in the guardhouse. I need them for my nerves."

Delancey ignored him. "Where?" he asked the cop.

The cop gave the watchman a prod and the drunk man led them among the sky-high heaps of waste, still lamenting and pleading. The small legs of the dead child were the first thing

Delancey saw. The rest of the body was obscured by an old defunct refrigerator.

"God damn it," said Ayser and stopped.

"Take him away, he's hard on the ears," Delancey told the cops, and they pulled away the watchman. Delancey walked up to the body. It was a girl, around six years old, with her hands tied with electrical tape.

"One less kid to look for," Delancey said.

It was little Sandy Hooper, the first child who went missing months ago on Stellen Street, where the kidnapper got its media moniker from. At least her parents would not be tortured by uncertainty anymore. But now Delancey knew he had to hurry even more. Each day of delay could mean another loss of a child's life. He looked down at his shoes and kept silent for a while. Finally, he lifted his head and said to Ayser:

"You can put down in the kidnapper's profile that he's probably a smoker."

"Why?"

Delancey pointed at the girl's arms. "Those are cigarette burns."

Snow began to fall, the snowflakes swirling in the light of sodium lamps illuminating the dumpsite, melting as soon as they landed on the ground.

It was dawn and the sky was turning pale when they were sitting in Ayser's car watching the coroner take away the body to the morgue. They were drinking from paper cups, Ayser drinking coffee with milk, Delancey herbal tea, and playing with the wet cord from the teabag. One of the cops had brought the drinks from the nearest gas station.

By the marks on the body, Delancey concluded the cause of death was strangulation, but of course they needed to wait for the proper results from the lab before they could be sure. The coroner drove away, taking the little body with him.

Ayser produced a metal hip flask from the glove compartment.

"Dad called it his medicine," he said without much humor, pouring a good amount of whisky into his coffee. "Want some, chief?"

Delancey shook his head.

"This is terrible," Ayser said, staring out the window at the piles of trash. "How could someone do such a thing? Makes you lose all will to live in this world, where such a thing is possible."

Delancey chortled. Ayser looked at him, surprised.

"What? You see a tortured kid and it makes no impression on you?"

Delancey looked at the tiny snowflakes glistening on the window.

"What impression would you like that makes on me? And what difference would that make?"

Ayser didn't answer, he was just looking at him with a frown.

"As you can see, it so happens we're living in a world where a man tortures and kills a little kid," Delancey said. "You're not going to get any other world. So what do you do? Sulk in a corner and think about impressions? Or try to make it a tiniest bit better?"

"But how can someone be so evil?" Ayser said. "This is what I can't grasp. Just the idea of it."

"Open your mouth," Delancey said. "Come on. Trust me."

Ayser opened his mouth warily. Delancey quickly reached out and grabbed one of his upper teeth. Ayser gasped in surprise.

"This! Here!" Delancey yelled. "Do you know what this is? It's a fang. A canine, if you will. Do you know what's it for? No? It's for killing and tearing flesh."

He let go of Ayser's tooth and wiped his fingers on his trousers.

"It's just some of us are trying to be guard dogs," Delancey continued. "This is my answer and it's enough for me."

Ayser was sitting there, sulking, and Delancey laughed again at the look on his face.

"*The world is evil!* Ugh. Did somebody high above ask you for your comments? Did somebody make you a critic of the world? Maybe you have a magazine column: 'Ray's Views on Creation?' The fact that you're born doesn't make you a judge of being. Instead, when you see something shitty, try to fix it. That's all there is to it."

He sipped the hot tea and thought for a while. "You won't find much sense in life elsewhere," he added.

Ayser sighed and shook his head.

"I want to go home," he said.

Delancey looked into his cup. It was almost empty, only some greenish, murky liquid remained at the bottom.

What did he have up till now? An anonymous email pointing them to a white van. A weird photo in which everyone saw a different face. And now the body. The body could be a treasure trove of evidence. Fingerprints, traces of the culprit's bodily fluids, residue from the place the victim was kept.

Somebody banged on the hood of their car and they looked up. It was the young cop.

"It's the guy's car..." he said.

They followed him to the old sedan next to the guardhouse. The trunk was open. Among a sea of mint wrappers, there was a large bag, dark with blood, and a Barbie doll, her dress shining with sequins.

"He swears it's the first time he's seen those," the young cop said.

"Wow," Ayser said, and looked at Delancey. "Seems we have our man!"

But the look on Delancey's face told Ayser he was far from being so sure.

In the morning, Gabriel sat down at the kitchen table. His mother put a plate in front of him, an omelet and orange juice.

"You're not eating?" he asked her.

"I already did," his mother said.

He knew she didn't eat, but didn't want him to be worried. He tried to eat the omelet even though morsels of food were getting stuck in his tightened throat and he had to wash them down with juice.

In those days there were some short moments when he could think about something else than the kidnapping. Small things of everyday life: a bath, a toast, a bus. But then, at once, a bitter reflux kept coming up, making everything empty and devoid of hope: *Matt is gone. His room is empty.*

He spent the whole night wandering the city, asking demons about his brother. But nobody had seen Matt or the white van. The trace ended at Constitution Square.

"It's time to go," he said.

His mother looked away from her silent phone and stared at her older son. She nodded.

"Just please ... be careful."

"I will, Mom."

"And, and ... please call me when you get there."

"I will."

As he was riding to school on his bike, with Maurice moving through the air beside him, they passed by the old playground. The equipment was already taken down, metal pipes lying on the ground, construction workers tearing up the rubber mulch off the ground.

"I owe you my life," Maurice said, floating beside Gabriel.

. . .

THE WORD about Matt's disappearance must have gotten out. He felt it in the way other students were looking at him. They seemed embarrassed. They didn't know what to say. Most kids aren't good with giving each other reassurance and keeping each other's spirits up. Only Martin was trying to talk to him about regular stuff, to make him laugh, but as he failed he gradually stopped bothering him, realizing all the time he had spent ranting to the camera making YouTube videos didn't prepare him for his best friend's tragedy.

"Send me Matt's photo, I will post it on my channel," he said. "I have followers all around. Maybe somebody's seen him."

"Thanks."

At school, Gabriel felt himself slip into some kind of warm lethargy. School was relaxing in this way. He knew he couldn't do anything in these walls. It was a strictly controlled environment, so he just sat there, happy that he could finally get a modicum of rest.

When algebra started, Ms. Holloway stopped at his table.

"The calculus test is today," she said. "Maybe you want to take it some other time."

He'd totally forgotten. The test that his stipend depended on.

"No, that's okay," he said, afraid that even though he wasn't studying, they would take his stipend away if he postponed it.

"Please close your books," said Ms. Holloway as she stood by the whiteboard.

Among sighs and silent moans, the students prepared for the test. Ms. Holloway put a sheet of paper with printed questions on his desk. Gabriel looked on, as others were busily leaning over their tests and penning in their answers. It seemed so ridiculous, so unimportant in the face of Matt's abduction. He stared at the questions and realized he couldn't solve a single one. They seemed abstract, all those strange symbols, so distant from his real-life problems.

Ms. Holloway was looking at him. It'd been twenty minutes and he hadn't written a thing. He thought about his mother, the worry in her eyes, her pale face. He felt angry at her that she was so powerless, and gave up so easily. He picked up his pen and pointed with it at his textbook.

"Come out," he whispered.

The demon of the textbook was a strict woman with round glasses on her thin nose.

"Solve those," he whispered to the demon of the textbook.

Ms. Holloway shot him a stare from across the classroom.

"Gabriel? Who are you talking to?"

"Myself."

The demon of the textbook took a deep breath and she started:

"X equals one..."

There. At least Mom would have a son who was best in class. Gabriel wrote so fast his wrist ached.

"Go on," he whispered to the Textbook.

Ms. Holloway walked up to Gabriel's desk. He seemed to be completely lost in thought, answering question after question. She couldn't see any way he might be cheating. No headphones, no cellphone, no papers hidden anywhere.

As the class ended, and the students turned in their papers and were packing their bags, Andrea was waiting for Gabriel in the hall.

"I've heard what happened," she said.

He looked at her and just nodded. It was obvious he didn't want to talk.

"I ... if I could help in any way, just say, okay?" Andrea said.

"Yes," he said and took his bag and walked away. "Thank you."

She watched him leave. She wanted to help him, but she didn't know how.

. . .

Gabriel went to the vending machine and told its fat, dreamy demon to give him a Mars bar. He watched as the machine spun its inner mechanisms and the bar fell into the hatch. Was that stealing? He wasn't sure. He wanted to walk away with the bar, but a guilty conscience made him come back and put a coin on the top of the machine.

Physical education was next. They were playing basketball. Before the game, Gabriel had a word with the demon of the ball, a super tall, joyful man. Gabriel wasn't a great player: he was fast, but lacked the aggression necessary to push through the other players and score. But on that day, the coach and the other players couldn't believe what they saw. None of the balls Gabriel threw missed their target. He scored seemingly impossible throws from the other side of the court. He didn't even have to try too hard. He just had to throw the ball strong enough and the demon made all necessary corrections to its trajectory to make sure it went straight down through the hoop.

When he was changing his clothes after the game, taking off his t-shirt moist with sweat, his phone screen lit up. It was a new tweet from the local news syndicate he followed to be on the lookout for any news about the investigation.

Kidnapped Child Found Dead, it said.

"No..." whispered Gabriel. His friends looked at him in surprise. They had known little Matt. He used to show up at their school from time to time, always with Gabriel's mother.

Half-naked, Gabriel covered his mouth with his fist, holding back a cry of despair. He took his phone and his trembling thumb hovered over the screen, afraid to open the tweet and see the news that would break his heart forever. He clenched his teeth so hard it hurt. And with one swipe of his thumb, he opened the news.

Girl. A girl. Not Matt. Another child. Not Matt.

He dropped on the bench and covered his face. The other

boys were leaving the locker room in silence, their heads hung low, their mouths silent.

"GABRIEL, PLEASE COME HOME..." The voice of his mother in his phone was quiet. "I'm worried that..."

"I'm not going missing," said Gabriel, looking from the corner at six police cruisers in front of the station. Maurice was beside him, listening with interest to the human conversation of mother and son. She went quiet. Gabriel could hear her breathing.

"I would just prefer it if you were with me ... during this ... time."

"He kidnaps little kids," Gabriel said.

Joan was quiet for a while. Then she said: "Just please be home before dark."

"I will see," Gabriel answered and disconnected.

"They're a tough bunch," Maurice said, looking at the cruisers. "They take their duty very seriously."

"But they have to listen to me, no?" Gabriel asked. "You said every thing knows the Great Covenant and the Sign, right?"

Maurice didn't seem completely sure.

"We will see," he said without much conviction.

Finally, everybody was gone from the parking lot, and Gabriel moved to the front of the fenced gate.

"Come out, you all!" he commanded.

Six demons of the police cars, uniformed and serious, materialized in the lot, hovering above their cruisers, and stared at Gabriel.

"Show us your ID!" demanded the one closest to Gabriel. "What are you doing here, citizen? We protect and we serve and we demand your ID, though you have the right to remain silent and call your lawyer!"

"Here is my ID," Gabriel said and made the Sign of the Covenant.

"Ah ... this..." The demons looked at each other. They were uncomfortable with the Ombudsman being here.

"Here we live by law and order," said one of the demons. "We don't like that spiritual, highfalutin stuff."

"But you have to listen to me. I am the Ombudsman," Gabriel said.

There was no disagreement. Gabriel looked to the side to comment to Maurice how their worries had been unnecessary, but Maurice was nowhere to be seen. Maybe as a street demon with an anarchistic nature, he didn't like the police.

"Last night, a dead child was found," Gabriel said to the demons. "But that's all the media says."

"Good thing! They would interfere with the investigation! Damn libtard journos will do anything to make us look bad," the demons commented.

"But I have to know where that was. Where was the child found?"

A chubby, mustachioed demon moved to the front.

"I was the one on the scene!" he exclaimed. "Aye, son, that was me there who carried the officers on their dutiful tasks!"

"I asked where it was."

The demon went silent. He was obviously hesitating.

"In ... in the interest of investigation..." he tried to protest, but Gabriel stared at him firmly.

"I am the Ombudsman, and I know the Sign of the Covenant, and I command you, demon!"

The demon growled at him quickly. "I'm telling! I'm telling! There's no need for that argument. On the outskirts of the city that was, in that dump, Danube Street 127! Are you happy, son?"

Gabriel put down the address in the maps app on his phone. The app showed him the location of the dump and a photo of high heaps of trash.

"Just ... please," the demon pleaded. "Don't use what I told you to hinder the investigation."

"On the contrary. You have aided the investigation very much," Gabriel answered.

The demon smiled radiantly. He was very happy to hear that.

MAURICE WAS WAITING for Gabriel by his bicycle, hidden behind the wall.

"Why were you hiding?" Gabriel asked him.

"Cops make me nervous," Maurice explained. "I like freedom and having fun. All that talk of law and order depresses my free spirit."

Gabriel checked the map again.

"There's a long way before us," he said. "I hope your free spirit likes dumps."

8

LAMENT OF THINGS

IT WAS FIVE MILES. Gabriel rode through the suburbs with their nice houses and gardens, and then it was warehouses and chop shops, and used car dealerships. He discovered he could order the demon of his bike, Giovanni, to go on its own. He didn't even have to use the pedals, but that felt weird. The bike was going very smoothly now, and Giovanni helped Gabriel uphill.

He passed by a huge home improvement warehouse and then it was just forest. He was riding in a bike lane on the side of an empty street. It was very silent and calm in the forest. He could only hear the wind and the hum of his bike wheels.

And then in the silence he started to hear a quiet, strange sound: like a choir of a thousand voices, all wailing and talking over each other, a grieving hum, growing louder and louder.

The forest ended and he stopped so rapidly he almost fell off his bike. He saw the dump. Mountains of trash rose above the chain-link fence, one by one, glistening in bright sunlight. But that was nothing. At the feet of the heaps of waste, a countless crowd of impoverished, emaciated demons wailed and complained, raising their arms to the sky. The noise was deafening.

"What's going on?" he asked Maurice.

But before Maurice could reply, the demons behind the fence noticed Gabriel. They started to reach toward him and wave at him, crying:

"Help me, oh, Seer! My body is broken!"

"Give me a new life!"

"Seer, don't make me die!"

Maurice was saying something, but Gabriel couldn't hear him over the deafening lament.

"Please, be quiet! Don't talk at once!" he cried at the demons, without effect. Finally, he made the Sign of the Covenant and yelled: "Shut up! I am the Ombudsman!"

And there was silence. He rode up to the fence and pointed at one of the demons, a man with ragged clothes and bulbous eyes.

"You. There was a dead child found last night somewhere around here. You know anything about this?"

"I saw no child," answered the demon. "In here it's just rot and death and destruction without hope."

"Anyone?" Gabriel looked at the dirty, thin faces.

"I did," said an old, bearded man. "I am the oldest one here. My totem and home is this vacuum cleaner, still amazing and powerful, more so than the modern products, broken easily, with weak suction, with newfangled gadgets that are pure marketing ploy—"

"I'm not here to listen about vacuum cleaners," Gabriel interrupted him. "Speak to me about the child."

"It was found on the other side of the main lane," said the Vacuum Cleaner, and pointed behind him with a trembling, thin hand. "Over there the horrid find took place, and officers of law gathered there last night."

"Thank you," Gabriel nodded at the demon and rode down along the fence to the gate.

In front of the gate stood a thick man in gray coveralls, with a red nose that looked like a cauliflower. He was looking at

Gabriel with his angry, squinted eyes. Gabriel stopped under the stare.

"What the fuck do you think you're doing here?" the man said in a coarse voice. Gabriel realized the man wasn't another demon. His skin was reddish and had no trace of that deathly pale blue color the demons had.

"Who are you?" Gabriel asked carefully.

"Santa Claus," said the man, and spat green phlegm next to Gabriel's feet. "Now you answer me. What are you doing here, huh? Are you a halfwit?"

"What...?"

"A half-wit, a retard, right? Talking to the trash?"

"I, uh, I was talking to myself," Gabriel said. "I just remembered something."

The man was just staring at Gabriel in silence. Gabriel felt afraid. He thought that the man might be the kidnapper.

"I have to go," Gabriel said in a faint voice.

"Tell you what, that's a good idea. So now why don't you get on that flashy bike of yours and fuck off and stop wandering around here, huh? How about that?"

Gabriel nodded, turned his bike around and rode away. He stopped in the distance and took a look behind him. The man was entering a little guardhouse next to the gate, where he shut the door behind him.

Gabriel turned to a small, shivering lady, the demon of a broken hairdryer. Her hair was standing straight up, surrounding her head like a halo.

"Who was that man? The one with the funny nose?"

"The drunken fool!" exclaimed the demon. "Our second watchman. He watches over this field of broken dreams and despair. Sits in his cabin watching pornography and imbibing cheap potato alcohol!"

"I see," Gabriel said.

"Usually he's here only at day, and the other watchman is

here at night. But the other one was taken by the police. So we're stuck with this brute."

"Thank you."

Gabriel crossed the street and rode up to the gate again, paying attention to not being seen from the barred windows of the guardhouse. He pointed at the guardhouse door.

"Lock and door, come out!" he whispered.

As soon as the demons of the door and lock appeared, he made the Sign and said: "The door must be locked with no way of opening! Lock, keep the door strong! Door, don't budge from place!"

He left his bike at the gate and he entered the dump. As he was passing the guardhouse, he saw the watchman's surprised face in the window. The door rattled as the man tried to open it, then he started thumping on it manically, shouting, "Let me out! Let me out now!" as Gabriel went on, passing the lines of hungry, poverty-stricken demons of defunct products thrown out from the city.

"They lead their pitiful half-lives here, heaps upon heaps of unneeded appliances," Maurice was telling Gabriel as they were moving deeper and deeper into the site, between two mountains of waste. "They carry on as long as their totem is still usable and able to function as intended, hoping someone comes by and takes them to work again. But in vain. As the rust and rot has its say, their totems will crumble and fall apart. And along with it, their existence."

"Where was the body?" Gabriel asked the line of demons and walked on, following their outstretched hands and pointing fingers.

Several demons were talking in hushed tones and squatting around one area by a mountain of debris. They stood up as they saw the Ombudsman and parted to let him pass, even though their bodies were no obstacle for him. Inside the circle of concerned demons, on the asphalt, there was a chalk-drawn outline of a small child.

Gabriel kneeled at its feet and kept silent for a while. Then he asked the demons:

"Who did it?"

There was silence. And then the demons began talking in unison, telling him about a strange man in a military jacket, with a white mask covering his face, who came here on a moonlit night with a large bag on his back, and the bag was dark and wet with blood. He opened the bag and threw the little body to the heap of trash and he stood there with the empty bag in his hands, a doll in a sequined dress sticking out of the pocket of his jacket, and the doll was crying over the death of its owner.

Then the man put his hand into his pocket and took out a pack of cigarettes, lifted the mask so that only his thin pale lips were visible, and he smoked a cigarette over the body. And then he left, and from one demon to the next, they told Gabriel that the killer arrived in a white van and left in the white van. And then the night watchman came and found the child and called the police.

"But I saw something more, yes I did!" said the demon of broken headphones whose only right headphone worked, and he kept his head tilted to one side.

"What?" Gabriel asked.

"When the man ... when the man took out his cigarettes," the demon said, "a small thing fell out, unseen. He didn't see the small thing!"

"What was that thing?"

"I didn't see well. A white paper. White small paper."

Gabriel started to search on the ground. A glint of something white caught his stare. There was a ticket.

"Come out," Gabriel ordered.

The demon of the ticket was small and humble. He considered himself very unimportant, and with each move and word he seemed to say he was sorry he existed.

"I am the humble, simple demon of a small ticket. Present me to a controller to gain possibility of travel, as a proof you have paid for the privilege of mass transportation," he said quietly. "Yesterday I was bought on subway station Demianov in the city center. I lived with a hundred of my brothers, in the dark innards of the ticket machine, until an unseen force spat me out into the evil man's hardened palm. He validated me in the subway gate."

"He was on the subway yesterday? Where did he go?" Gabriel asked.

"I was validated at the gate to line C-17, then he just stuffed me deep into the pocket of his jacket and I didn't see nor hear anymore, I'm sorry!" the ticket said. "I slept there, next to the pack of cigarettes and a lighter, until the night he dropped me here. I'm sorry."

"But he came here in a van?" Gabriel asked the demons. "Why did he need a subway ticket if he has a car?"

"There are many reasons people who have cars use public transport," Maurice pointed out. "Maybe he was just going somewhere where it was hard to find a parking spot. Or his car was broken. Or, or, or..."

Gabriel nodded. That was a good point. He thought for a while. What did he know? That the kidnapper came to the dumpsite in his white van, in his mask, and dropped the body here. And then he did what?

"What did the man do after dropping the body here? Where did he go?" he asked the demons of the dump.

"Then he went to the place where the night watchman keeps his car!" The Headphones remembered, pointing to the spot.

"Thank you." Gabriel nodded and was about to leave, when the demon of the headphones stopped him.

"Please," the Headphones said quietly, putting his hands

together in a begging gesture. "I told you what you wanted. Can you please take me from here? Can you please take me?"

"I'm sorry," Gabriel said. "I wouldn't know what to do with you..."

"You can still listen to the music with me!" said the demon. "A song sounds the same when you hear it with one ear! Maybe even better, you can concentrate more ... or you can hear danger with the other ear..."

Gabriel sighed, reached out and put the headphones in the pocket of his hoodie. Seeing that, the other demons started to cry one over another:

"Me, too! You can use me, too! Take me with you, Ombudsman!"

"Shut up! We have to go," Maurice said.

"Sorry, I can't go around carrying a pile of things," Gabriel said, and they left the chalk outline. They went to the night watchman's car. The doors and trunk were sealed with police tape.

"Come out."

The demon of the watchman's car was a hardened woman in a checkered, flannel shirt.

"What, again?" she yelled. "Will I get no rest? Where is my owner and driver, the serious lonely man I know and serve?"

"What happened last night? Who put that tape on you?" Gabriel asked.

"The pigs, who else!" the demon yelled. "They found those strange things inside me and they grabbed my owner and driver, put handcuffs on his hands! But those weren't his things!"

"What things?" Gabriel asked.

"An empty bag, large and rough, and a little girl's doll. This is what they found in me, and for what they took my owner away, but what is the crime in having a bag and a toy? What evil sin could that be? The pigs! Curse their eyes!"

"The bag in which the dead child was brought here," Maurice said to Gabriel.

"If those weren't your owner's things, how did they end up inside you?" Gabriel asked.

"The strange man put them inside me."

Gabriel and Maurice exchanged looks.

"He knew that stupid smelly sign," the demon of the car said. "He ordered me to open my trunk even though it was locked! He put those evil items in me, told me to lock up and he left! And thus he brought misery upon my owner, of that I'm sure!"

"The real kidnapper framed the night watchman," Maurice said.

"Are those things still inside you?" Gabriel asked.

"The pigs took them. And then they took fingerprints from all parts of my body. Why my owner didn't shoot them dead, I don't know! How many hours have we spent on the road together, listening to songs about endless travel and heartbreak. I want him back! Set him free!"

"And what did the strange man do then? Did you see?" Gabriel asked.

"He sneaked out of the site and drove away ... in a shitty old van, Ford E-Series."

"Did you see the plates on the van?"

"No."

"Ombudsman!" Gabriel heard Giovanni's cry in the distance. He looked to the fence. The demon of his bike was waving his hands in the air.

"Police! They're coming here!" Giovanni yelled.

"Let's go!" Gabriel snapped to Maurice and they rushed to the gate.

Demons of discarded things were yelling after him: "Don't forget about us, Seer! Don't leave us here, forgotten, destined to die! Remember us, Ombudsman! Take me with you! Take me! I am still useful! I helped you, so help me! I told you about the evil man at night! Take me from here!" The noise was deafening. Gabriel covered his ears and ran across the dump back to his bike outside.

"Over there!" Giovanni said, pointing down the street.

A police cruiser was coming. Gabriel could see the cops inside staring at him. It had crossed his mind before that the police wouldn't leave a crime scene like that. And here they were. He stepped on the pedals hard and they left the dump behind them, the lament of discarded things growing quieter the further they went away, toward the city.

"Are they following us?!" he asked Giovanni.

The demon looked behind. "They pulled over at the gate."

"Charming little place," Maurice shuddered, hovering next to the moving bike. "We didn't get much from there, did we? Hard to say what to do next."

"Wrong," Gabriel said, looking towards the thin, misty scepters of the city skyline on the horizon, where the road was taking them.

"What?"

"We've got this," Gabriel said. He put his hand into his pocket, took something out and showed it to Maurice. The little, dirty subway ticket.

9

THE HEAT

Delancey was sitting at his desk in the light of a small lamp, eating a hamburger. His shirt open, he felt sweat trickle down his chest. The AC hadn't been functioning for days, and the hot wind from the bay was falling through the open windows. The weather was definitely going crazy this April. One day it was freezing and snowing, the other it was hot as hell. The whole Bay Area seemed to lie at the center of recent climate anomalies.

The rest of the floor was engulfed in darkness. From his desk, through the windows of his office, Delancey could see the distant, blinking red lights: warning beacons on the tops of sky-high cranes of the industrial port.

There was a ping and the screen of his computer came alive with light. Delancey put aside his hamburger and logged in. He had new mail.

From: The Ombudsman. You have the wrong man. The night watchman was framed. The real kidnapper who killed that little girl is using not only his white van for transport but also the subway, specifically line C-17.

Delancey cursed under his breath and grabbed the phone from his desk.

"Are you out of your mind, Delancey? It's 10 PM," said the angry voice of Marilyn, their IT specialist.

"I got another email from that Ombudsman fellow. I suppose your brilliant experts have identified the source of emails already?"

"I thought you got your man today?"

"I thought I asked you to check those emails."

"Listen, man, some of us have homes and families to spend evenings with," snapped Marilyn. "It's done when it's done. You'll be the first to know."

"When?"

"Excuse me, I'm going to go and read my children a goodnight story now that we've caught the kidnapper and we can all sleep calm at night."

She disconnected. *They got their man* ... didn't they? Only another mysterious email from an unknown ... but very knowledgeable ... sender claimed otherwise. There was movement and a shadow, and Delancey looked up. Ayser was standing in the door.

"He's ready for another session," Ayser said.

Delancey nodded, stood up and grabbed his wallet and phone from the desk. They went to the staircase and Delancey had to squint because it was filled with white, artificial light.

"Who knows he's here?" he asked Ayser.

"What do you mean? From the department?"

"No, I mean ... outside."

"The press release is tomorrow," Ayser said. "Today was just the news about the body."

Delancey nodded, deep in thought, as they went down the stairs.

"Why are you asking?"

"Nothing."

Delancey hated the underground detainment level. He was

suffocating in there. Low ceilings, plastic furniture, fluorescent lamps.

The night watchman looked at them with fear as they entered the interrogation room. His large, hairy hands were trembling. He was still in his dirty working clothes.

"Let's pick up where we left," Delancey said, leaning against the table with his fists.

"I didn't do it," the watchman whispered.

"Yes, I think it's pretty accurately where we left," Delancey said. "You didn't kill the girl, you just found her and called the police, and your fingerprints on her clothes appeared there by magic, I suppose."

"I didn't know she was dead. I wanted to help her."

"Is that what you usually do? You see a dead body, you pick it up?"

"I don't know!" the watchman cried. "I just did." He was staring at them with the desperation of an unintelligent man caught in an intrigue he couldn't understand. "I just guard the dump. That's what I do."

"And the bag and the doll? You picked them up, too, and put them into your car for safekeeping?"

"I don't know how they got there."

"We had to unlock your car to search it. It was locked. Those things were inside. So, please tell me, who else has the keys to your car?"

"Nobody has the keys to my car."

"That follows, doesn't it, that anyone who wanted to put the bloody bag and the toy, identified by the parents of the dead girl as her possession, that person must have had the keys to your car. And seeing that the only person with the keys was you..."

Delancey leaned closer to the terrified face. He could smell the acrid odor of the watchman's body.

"Well, what follows is that it must have been you. Is my logic flawed?"

The watchman clenched his jaw and shook his head. Delancey sighed and stood up.

"Who is 'the ombudsman?'" he asked.

The watchman shrugged.

"It's the first time I heard..."

"Who sends me emails? Saying you're innocent? Pretty convenient, huh?"

A dry, crying spasm shook the watchman's body. He lowered his head and hid his face in his hands.

"I don't know what you're talking about!"

Fury overcame Delancey and he slapped the man's forehead with his open hand. The watchman's head jerked back and he looked up at Delancey with teary eyes. Delancey raised his fist, ready to smash the watchman's nose.

"Where are you keeping the rest of the kids?" he yelled. "Where are the children you took?"

"Andrew..." Ayser said.

Delancey regained control, sighed and lowered his fist. He stared at the watchman.

"I just found the girl at my dump ... and I just called you," the watchman said, his eyes begging Delancey to trust him.

"We have enough to sentence you for life, you know," Delancey answered.

His phone rang. He was being called to the director's office. As he was leaving, in the doorway, he heard the night watchman break into tears, his face hidden in his palms, his shoulders trembling, tears dropping down to the hard plastic table.

"You're going to have to wipe that," Delancey said and left.

As always, when he visited his boss in his office, he smelled stale cigarette smoke. It was no different this time. It was obvious that Boleani, known for his perfect conduct, had to smoke in secret, but he was never caught. And as always, Delancey looked around for an ashtray or a trace of smoke. Where Boleani had been putting out his cigarettes was a big mystery to the agents of their department.

Boleani got up from behind his desk when he saw Delancey.

"Andrew, please, tell me we have it."

Delancey thought about it and saw no point in telling his boss about his doubts. He had nothing to back them up.

"We still don't have the rest of the kids," he said.

"It's true," Boleani nodded. "That's our priority now. To find out where the children are being held."

"One thing I'm still missing..." Delancey said hesitantly.

Boleani wrinkled his eyebrows over the child-like blue eyes. "What?"

"I'm getting information from an unknown source that's hard to trace. You know there's a lot of crazy people, especially in a media case like this. But I have a feeling there's more to it. An anonymous informant has described the kidnapper's clothing in accordance with what we have from the security camera at the preschool. And now there's another word from him about a white van that the kidnapper supposedly took away Matt in."

Boleani listened to him carefully, squinting.

"What do we have on that car?"

"We've got pictures of a white van passing by the preschool at a similar time. But we can't see the license plates."

"Can you see the driver?"

Delancey hesitated. He shrugged. "A blurry man. The quality is too poor."

"I see."

"Anyway. There's no trace of the van at the dumpsite, or anywhere near the night watchman's home. He was driving an old sedan. And it was in the sedan that we found the girl's doll and the bag."

"But listen to yourself. You found the kidnapped girl's

belongings in the trunk of his car. You're not done yet? I think it's stronger evidence than anonymous emails."

"Stronger," Delancey nodded. "No doubt about it."

"Send me these pictures, I'll take a look at them," said Boleani. "But focus on the watchman. We need to know where the children are."

"Of course, boss."

Boleani was staring at him and finally said: "What do you do to stay so lean? I'm vegan for ten years and still flabby. Are you on some kind of a diet?"

Delancey looked at his reflection in the full-size wall mirror in the distant corner of the room. Since he had realized he was ugly, which had happened pretty early in his life, he never paid much attention to mirrors. But now he could see he'd grown even thinner. *Yeah, my diet comes in tiny syringes*, he thought.

"I guess it's just genes," he said.

"Must be," Boleani nodded. "Try going vegan, Andrew. You'll feel better, and animals will thank you too."

At the same moment, Gabriel was lying in his bed looking at the silhouette of Maurice, who was leaning out through the window, staring into the distance.

"What are you doing?"

Maurice didn't turn his head.

"Listening to the voices of the city," the demon answered calmly. "Listening to the news from the streets. They grow louder at night, when the city goes to sleep, and I can hear them better, without the racket of man and traffic drowning everything in their noise. So I'm asking and listening. Maybe someone saw the masked man and we don't have to spend another day in the subway."

That was a jab at Gabriel. After getting back from the dump, he had bought a day pass and rode C17 for hours, from station to station, looking at faces of passengers, looking for the man who took his little brother. There were twenty-one stations in the C17 line, and Gabriel visited each of them: the end of the line, where the city ended and a natural reserve started; Rektov District, a dangerous slum with lean, angry looking inhabitants; Lakoff with villas and gardens; the projects of Arch Triumphal where the housing blocks rose high up to the sky; the business district of Flote Street...

He wore down his feet. He asked the subway trains and station benches and cameras. Nobody remembered the big man in a military jacket, army boots and a mask.

"I can't ask the demons about the mask," Gabriel said suddenly in his bed.

"Eh?"

"He can't be wearing the mask in public. Everyone would stare at him. He can't want that," Gabriel said.

Maurice turned back from the window.

"Heard anything?" Gabriel asked him.

"News from Bombay, news from Moscow, news from far away," Maurice answered. "There is unrest in the world, political turmoil, movement of angry masses, and hordes marching. Secret coded messages from government agencies crossing the sky. But no word of Matt."

"Gabriel? Son...?" there was his mother's voice at the door.

"Yes?"

The door opened and she came in, wearing her red bathrobe. His pale, worried mother. It still struck him that she couldn't see Maurice standing five feet from her, nor any of the demons. It made him feel lonely.

"What do you want, Mom?"

"I just wanted to see you. You're away from home so often. I'm worried."

"What good would be sitting home and crying?"

She couldn't answer. She nodded, finally.

"I don't want to lose you, too, Gabriel," she said. "I look at you and I see a man. Not my boy anymore. You've changed in these days ... and it breaks my heart seeing you so."

Gabriel wanted to scream at her, angry at her empty, aimless hysteria, her soft feelings, but he managed to control himself. He stood up in his t-shirt and trunks and approached his mother.

"I promise you, you don't have to worry about me. I'm happier this way, looking for him. I would die sitting at home, like you, and ... and ... drowning in despair. Is this what you want for me?"

She shook her head and bit her lip. Her eyes shone with tears. He embraced her. They were the same height now, and they stood embracing in the dark room, high above the city. Maurice coughed and turned his eyes away, apparently embarrassed at this show of human emotion.

Gabriel could hear the beating of his mother's heart. He remembered a video he saw once and it made a big impression on him, about the mother's heartbeat being the sound that a human child learned first, back in the womb. Those low, double beats, bringing safety, always there. When all the child saw was dim reddish light coming through the skin of her belly, and all the child heard was the beating of her heart: "I'm here. I'm here." And when the children are born, at the time of the great division, the doctors put them on their mother's breast and they can still hear her heartbeat coming through her flesh and ribs. But at that time it already sings a different song: "Goodbye. Goodbye." Gabriel felt uncomfortable with this odd vision, clenched his jaw and gently pushed his mother away from him.

"Goodnight, Mom," he said.

IT WAS dark when Delancey was going by bus to his one-bedroom apartment in Ursenev, a distant residential district, full of identical high-rises. He had a car, an old Mercedes, but he rarely drove it. He liked his long meditations in public transport. It's not like he had a lot to do at home. On the bus, he was sitting by the window, watching the mating dance of young people on the streets in downtown. Made up, beautiful, fashionably dressed, they were ready to go on a date, for a drink in a club, for an all-night disco.

The senior agent felt different from other humans. He had a secret that few people knew. Andrew Delancey was not his real name. And his family tree was quite complicated, its branches interlocked in ways that took a longer while to comprehend.

He was a son of his grandfather and a brother of his mother. Or, you could say he was a grandson of his father and a son of his sister. It was so confusing that in his case the oldest and safest environment in the world, the family, became a meaningless, scary cobweb of incest and abuse.

He spent the first five years of his life underground.

At fifty-years-old, Per Lipshitz had kept his mentally-disabled daughter locked in the basement. Interrogated years later, he would say he wanted to protect her from the evil world outside. Instead, he made her his sexual toy. His wife probably knew about it, but the subject never came up. She was mainly interested in alcohol; the disappearance of her demanding daughter didn't bother her. And so Lipshitz's daughter got pregnant by her own father and gave birth to a boy. They never even gave him a name.

He lived in the basement. Neither his crazy mother nor Lipshitz were good to him. His sister-mother sometimes played with him and hugged him, and sometimes she beat him. He never knew what was coming. He still had scars on his thighs from the one time she struck him with a fire poker.

Then, one fateful night, Lipshitz had an argument with his wife, and on the next day she reported him to the police. Lipshitz went to jail, his daughter went to an institution, and the little boy ended up in a state-run children's home, where they gave him a name. It was like a second birth for him.

Andrew was the name of the orphanage director's late father. Delancey was the surname of an actress who was very popular at that time. It turned out to be quite ironic, as the actress was beautiful and the boy was anything but. Thanks to the name, though, nobody could connect him with the shocking story of abuse and incest.

He crawled out from darkness into the world of light and color. Everything was better than those five years in the basement. He loved the world outside. But soon he felt he was not a part of it and he could never be. He was tainted by his origin. Born out of such unnatural coupling, was he even human? His grandfather was his father. His sister was his mother. Other kids were getting adopted, but there was something in him that scared prospective parents and he remained in the children's home until he came of age. Even though he tried to guard the shameful secret of his origin, people somehow knew that he was different.

When he realized he would never have a real home, a real family, he wanted to die. But then he discovered what he could do. A man from the dark basement, he could stand on the border between light and darkness and guard it. He was not happy ... but he had a purpose. That, in his opinion, was more important. Straight after high school, he went to the police academy, then moved on to NBI. Without a private life to speak of, he moved up in the ranks faster than any other recruit.

Back home, in his tiny apartment, Andrew Delancey lowered all the blinds until the living room started to look like a bunker, cut off from the world. He could only sleep in total darkness. He used the bedroom only when there was someone else with him. He didn't like to sleep on a bed. He used to lie on the sofa instead, because he liked to have the soft support from one side, as if there was someone sleeping with him.

He thought about the night watchman, crying in the interrogation room. Tomorrow they would get back to him.

He lay there and listened to the loud ticking of the clock and the hum of the plumbing in the walls. He had a feeling he wouldn't sleep that night without help. He jumped out of bed and went to the bathroom, naked, to inject himself with morphine.

10

METRO PANIC

The next day after school, as Gabriel chained his bike to a post next to the subway station and walked down the stairs to the platform, Maurice groaned.

"Not again."

"I thought you were supposed to help me, not complain at each and every inconvenience," Gabriel answered calmly as he boarded the train.

He rode to the transfer station and switched lines to C-17. Again he traveled round and round in the train for hours, staring at other passengers' faces. The demon of the ticket stood beside him, looking out, ready to call out if he saw the man who had bought him.

Hours passed. Gabriel fell into some kind of trance, hypnotized by the steady hum of the train swishing up and down the line. The hundreds of human faces turned into a flesh-colored sea before his eyes. He looked at the monitor showing a stream of insipid advertisements, meant to convince the commuters that buying something might make their lives slightly more bearable. Gabriel noticed on the screen that it was 7 PM: time to go home if he wanted to get there before dark.

Just then he felt his phone vibrate in his pocket. His mom.

Apparently she had waited on calling him until the top of the hour. She asked him to come home. He told her he would be back soon.

"I love you," she said.

"Me too." Gabriel put the phone in his pocket, looked up and froze.

On the seat directly opposite his sat a large man surrounded by a halo of darkness. He had mud on his military boots and he was wearing a dirty green military jacket. He had a dark-red baseball cap on his head. There were five fresh scars running across his cheek and his nose, as if someone's little hand had scratched his face in a desperate fight for life. His eyes were covered with large, black sunglasses ... and yet Gabriel knew that the man was staring straight at him. The man's lips were forming a small, crooked smile.

The train was full of people, but they seemed to all disappear behind a wall of mist in the presence of the man. Gabriel sat there, terrified and spellbound like a rabbit in the face of a snake. He knew he'd found the kidnapper, the killer, the tormentor of lost children.

And he couldn't do anything.

The scarred man and Gabriel were the only ones on the train who weren't staring at their phones. Gabriel felt his teeth rattling against each other, a flush of cold, a flush of hot, and his hair standing on the nape of his neck. As the train continued down the line, the passengers began to disperse, getting out on stations in their districts.

He and the man remained, surrounded by fewer and fewer people.

The man kept smiling at Gabriel, as if that strange boy, hiding his pale, terrified face in the hood of his sweatshirt amused him.

Gabriel reached into his pocket and took out the ticket he found at the dump. He held it in his fingers and stared at it, afraid to look up at the man in the opposite seat. The last remaining people in the car stood up and walked to the door, ready to get out as soon as the train stopped. Gabriel looked at the automated station plan on the wall. That was the stop before the last.

Gabriel swallowed. He was paralyzed.

The train stopped and the last people got out of the car.

He remained there alone with the killer.

An alarm sound warned the passengers the door was about to close. Gabriel jumped to his feet and ran out of the car to the platform, and then he ran to the next car of the same train, with the warning buzz sounding in his ears as he jumped in at the last moment.

The train started going to the last station of the line.

This car was empty.

Gabriel quickly moved to the side so that the man couldn't see him through the windowed door between the cars.

He took out the ticket again and called out the demon.

"Was that him? The man who lost you at the dump, next to the body of the little girl?"

The demon of the ticket stared at Gabriel, pale and frightened. Then he slowly nodded his head.

Gabriel was fighting his own panic.

"Stay calm, Ombudsman," he heard Maurice's quiet voice. "He has no idea that you know who he is."

Gabriel nodded. He needed to stay calm. He needed to think of something.

"Don't look!" he yelled to the security camera in the car.

"Lower my voice," he whispered to the microphone in the call box and hit the emergency button.

"Subway security, can we help you? We can't see your car," said the operator's voice from the speaker.

"I am the Stellen Street Kidnapper!" Gabriel said to the microphone. "I've kidnapped all those children, and I've killed the little girl at the dump! I'm wearing a red baseball cap and a green jacket, and I'm wearing sunglasses!"

"Hello? Hello...?"

The train was slowing down. Gabriel saw the lights in the tunnel behind the windows. They were rolling into the last station, the end of the line.

"Train! Come out!" he yelled.

The demon of the train appeared before him, a respectable older man with a white mustache, wearing the uniform and cap of train services. Gabriel made the Sign.

"Keep all doors closed! Don't open them when we stop at the station!"

"Yes, Ombudsman!" the Train saluted him and disappeared.

The last squeal of the brakes—they stopped at the platform. Gabriel peeked through the door's window to the last car.

The man was standing at the train door, waiting for it to open. At first he was surprised—he looked impatiently to the left and right to see if the other doors opened. Then he pressed the button next to the door. Nothing. Then he said something—and Gabriel saw the demon of the train appear next to him.

The kidnapper was a Seer and an Ombudsman, just like him.

"Open the door!" Gabriel read his lips, those thin pale lips in the puffed, scarred face.

The doors in all cars opened at once ... and then black-clad security guards appeared on the platform, coming from the escalator. They were looking around, then they pointed at their train, and started walking toward it. And the kidnapper saw them, too.

"Go!" he yelled to the Train.

The train jerked and jumped, rushing full speed in the direction from which they came, and the sudden movement threw Gabriel against the door between the cars. The kidnapper looked and saw him in the window staring at him with wide, terrified eyes.

The train was rushing through the underground tunnel, the wind howling in the car as the doors were still open; newspapers and foam cups flew in the air.

Gabriel pushed himself away from the door between the cars and began to run away from the horrifying man. He ran towards the front of the train.

"Open!" he yelled to the door to the next car, when he heard a mechanical hiss and turned to see the door in the end of his car opening and the killer walking in, heading towards Gabriel.

The door to the next car opened and Gabriel ran. He ran against the wind in the train hurling through dark tunnels, and the kidnapper chased him, getting closer and closer.

"Lock all doors!" the man bellowed.

Gabriel crashed into the door to the next car and rolled down to the floor. He could only look on as the man stopped running, grinned, and began to walk towards him. The kidnapper smiled, showing his thin, gray teeth.

"No ... no..." Gabriel whispered. He was looking into the face of death.

And then BOOOM!—a collision stopped the train in a huge crash, the noise of tons of steel slamming into each other. A powerful force pushed Gabriel into the door and threw the kidnapper against the wall. Gabriel smashed the back of his head against the door. He lost consciousness.

"Ombudsman!" he heard an urgent whisper and opened his eyes. He hurt so much. There was ringing in his ears. Maurice leaned over him, looking at Gabriel with concern. "There's no time for napping."

As he scrambled to his feet, Gabriel heard screams and calls for help from outside. Those were coming from the injured passengers from the train they had crashed into. The exit doors to the car were opening one by one with mechanical hisses, a safety procedure.

And then someone grabbed Gabriel by his ankle. He looked down—the man was lying on the floor, holding his leg in an iron grip. His sunglasses had fallen off during the crash and now Gabriel could see his eyes. Light blue, they reminded him of a shark's eyes; there were black outlines around them, tattooed or drawn, which gave that swollen, scarred face with unshaven beard a creepy look.

"Who are you?" snarled the killer, and pulled Gabriel's leg so strongly that the boy fell down. "I will give you some love," he whispered and reached towards Gabriel's face with his long, serrated fingernails.

"Lights out!" Gabriel shouted, and it became pitch black. He used the man's momentary surprise to push him away with all the force he could muster in his arms and legs, he stumbled to his feet, evading the man's grabbing hands, and remembering where the doors were he jumped out of the train, to the dark subway track.

And he ran.

Crying in fear, he ran away from the crash, along the subway tracks, through the underground tunnel, passing small red emergency lights in the metal cages.

He was out of breath and felt the metallic taste of blood in his throat as he emerged from the black tunnel at a brightly-lit platform. Somebody grabbed his outstretched hands and they pulled him onto the platform. It was full of impatient, concerned commuters.

"There was an accident? You were there?" somebody asked him, but Gabriel didn't answer; he tore himself away from his rescuers, broke through the gates and ran up the stairs, falling and running again, until he was outside, by the entrance to an unknown subway station in an unknown district of the city, under a clouded, darkening sky.

He dashed through the streets until he was sure the killer wasn't following him. He threw himself on a bench and panted spasmodically, trying to catch his breath. As he tried to hide his face in his hands, he felt sharp pieces of broken glass sticking out of his bleeding fingers.

Maurice appeared next to him, looking at Gabriel with concern.

"Damn. Exactly why I hate subways," Maurice said. "Not many escape routes."

Gabriel stared at him for a while, just breathing, before he managed to say anything. His whole body was shaking.

"I want to go home," he said in a breaking voice.

Some passersby, some corporate managers returning home from their air-conditioned offices, looked with surprise at a bloodied, tired boy talking to the air. But Gabriel had stopped caring long ago, and the businessmen were in a hurry to relax with a beer after the stressful working hours.

THEY ATE their dinner in silence. His mother didn't notice anything out of the ordinary about him. She had enough trouble on her own, Gabriel figured. They were still talking about the subway accident on TV. The police were looking for a man in a green jacket and red baseball hat. So they didn't catch him, Gabriel thought. He got away.

He went to his room, took out the workbooks from his schoolbag, and did the homework with his wounded, bleeding hands. Some shards of glass from the windows of the train fell out of his hair down onto the pages of his notebook.

Doing the homework was easy, if monotonous: he asked questions to the demon of the textbook and wrote the answers in his workbook. He had to do it, because the demon of the pen couldn't write on her own without someone holding it, and the workbooks couldn't write in themselves. He felt like somebody's secretary.

When he went to bed and switched off the light, he turned to the shadow of the demon next to his bed, staring at him in silence.

"We've got him," Gabriel said.

"We've got him? What are you talking about?" Maurice replied. "We almost died down there."

"He wanted to get off at the last station. Which probably means that's where he lives. I'll go there and ask around."

Maurice chortled. "Have I already told you that you were going to surprise me many times, Ombudsman?"

Gabriel just looked at him, offering no comment.

"You were in a fatal train accident. A perverted murderer was this close to cutting your throat! And here you are, a teenage boy, saying, 'We've got him!' That is resilience, my boy."

"Is my little brother alive?" Gabriel asked.

Maurice hesitated. "Oh. I don't know..." he said sadly.

"Didn't those voices from the world, coming on the wind at night, tell you?"

"No."

"So you don't know?"

"I don't."

"Neither do I. He might get killed any minute now. And if not, he is going to spend every minute afraid, alone, tortured. I'm not going to break down and cry like my mother."

Maurice stared at him with a smile. Finally, he said:

"You need to rest."

Gabriel closed his eyes. He could hear his mother's quiet voice coming from her room. He knew what she was doing. He'd seen her before and knew that tone of voice. She was kneeling by her bed, hands clasped together, praying. For Matt.

"You are a demon," Gabriel said to Maurice without opening his eyes.

"Yes?"

"Do her prayers ... go anywhere? Is there anyone high above listening to her?"

Maurice snorted in amusement. "I'm a piece of string on your hand, Gabriel, and you ask me such great questions. I have no idea." There was a second of silence. "Nobody does."

11

WHERE SEAGULLS DINE

In the morning, Demianov Square was full of people on their way to work. At a stand in the shadow of the NBI building, Delancey bought one *cortado leche y leche* and one black coffee.

"Have you heard about the subway yesterday, Agent?" the vendor asked.

Delancey nodded.

"Crazy stuff," the vendor said. "This city's going to rats. It's the immigration, I tell you."

Delancey paused and looked at the vendor. "Ali, aren't you an immigrant yourself?" he asked.

"It's different," Ali shrugged. "I've been here for twenty years."

"Okay."

"Whole subway line is cut off. It's bedlam."

"Good thing I travel by bus," Delancey said, and paid Ali for coffee.

He grabbed two hot paper cups and walked towards the office building. The seagulls circled above the square. He could hear their plaintive cries.

. . .

In the dark, monumental vestibule of NBI Los Maines, Delancey stopped at the guard's station to talk to the sixty-year-old security guard he liked, Stanley. Delancey handed him the sweet *cortado.*

"On double espresso," he said and winked at the guard.

"Goddamnit, boy, you're a savior!" Stanley cried out, grabbing his coffee. "The only thing that spoils this moment is I know you'll be asking for a favor one day and I can't refuse."

"Don't sweat it," Delancey answered. "It's out of the pure goodness of my heart."

"Yeah, sure." Stanley took a sip and looked at Delancey. "You look good, Agent. You're in good shape. Do you run?"

"Only when I'm being shot at."

"Andrew!"

Delancey looked up in surprise. A familiar figure was running towards him from the elevators.

"What's up, Ayser?"

"He killed himself," Ayser said.

The metal door clanked and they entered the cell. Delancey carefully stepped around the puddle of urine and approached the naked feet dangling in the air and looked up. The night watchman hung from the light fixture on something that looked like a rope rolled from some kind of textile. He was naked, his body was swollen and white, save for the purple neck and face of a man who'd died from suffocation.

"How could that happen?" Ayser asked.

"It's his shirt," Delancey said. "He tore it and made the rope." He pointed at the camera in the corner. "Recordings?"

"I've already secured them. Didn't have time to watch in detail, but, well, he's hanging himself."

"Who was on duty? Lennox?"

"Mainer. Now he's crying like a toddler. Says he was distracted by a phone call."

Delancey looked around the cell. "Wait. What's that?"

There was a folded sheet of paper lying on the pillow on the bed. Delancey took the paper and unfolded it.

"*I know the world will never forgive me for what I've done,*" he read. "*The children are all dead. The last body is hidden by Pier 12. The rest I drowned in the ocean there. I pray not for forgiveness. I pray there is nothing on the other side and this is the end.*"

Delancey and Ayser looked at each other.

"Get a car," Delancey snapped.

THE HEAVY, leaden waves crashed against the concrete pier, and seagulls circled above them, crying, as Delancey and Ayser stood by an old deserted warehouse, looking at the body of another child. It was stuffed between metal barrels. A boy this time. Delancey recognized little Phillip Dufres.

"Tell Beatrice to notify his parents," Delancey said. "See those?" He pointed at the boy's legs, sticking out of his jean shorts. "Dog bites."

"Poor kid," Ayser said.

"Look here. Under his feet."

There was a wrapper from Balthuser Mints. Delancey chortled and shook his head. He rolled his eyes.

"How convenient," he said.

"What do you mean?" Ayser asked.

Delancey walked up to the burnt remains of the van parked behind the warehouse. It was completely done for. Just a metal shell. No seats, no upholstery. And of course no fingerprints.

"And here we have the van we were looking for," he said, and turned to greet a team of divers approaching him from their operations car.

Delancey and Ayser sat on the pier and looked at the divers going underwater. One of them emerged after several minutes. He held a small sneaker in his hands. Delancey shook his head.

"We'll find it's another missing child's shoe ... and that's all we're going to find here," he said to Ayser.

"What do you mean?"

"If there ever was a shadow of a doubt it wasn't the watchman, now I'm positive."

"With his suicide note? The van? And the mints? The same as he ate..."

Delancey just looked at him and Ayser stopped talking. Finally, the senior agent said:

"You know what's improving my humor, Ayser? That the real killer is so dumb or deluded to think we're going to fall for that. Remember the opening line from the suicide note?"

"Something about forgiveness?"

"Yeah. *I know the world will never forgive me for what I've done.* This is bullshit. The watchman could barely put together a sentence and now he writes like a college hipster with pretensions to literary fame. And here we find his favorite mints. And another victim's shoe. You know what we won't find here, Ayser?"

Ayser just stared at him in silence.

"We won't find any more kids."

"Why?"

"Because the real killer is still playing with them," Delancey said.

BACK AT THE HEADQUARTERS, for the tenth time Delancey was leaning close to the screen, intently watching the recording of the cell from last night. The night watchman was sitting on the bed, looking around with his frightened eyes. Now and then, he would nod his head.

"Looks like someone was talking to him," said Delancey. "No sound?"

Mainer, his eyes still red from crying, shook his head.

"We just have video. But the footage from the hallway shows no one was passing."

"Someone's talking to him," Delancey repeated. "Maybe through the speaker in the cell?"

"I'm the only one who's got a microphone here," said Mainer, and then he just fell apart: "I had no idea something like this could happen," he said, sobbing. "It was five in the morning. My cell phone rang, an unknown number. A strange voice started asking me about my family ... how my family is doing. I got scared, I asked what was going on and who was talking. I couldn't watch the screens. And when I looked back at them ... it was too late."

On the video, the night watchman took a piece of paper and started writing on it.

"Where did he get it from?" asked Delancey.

Mainer shook his head in silence.

"Professionals," Delancey muttered with contempt.

The night watchman took off his pants, and with his penis showing, he climbed up to the chair and dropped his pants on the camera, obscuring the view of the cell.

"Senior Agent Delancey. Please don't punish me. It's not my fault."

"Everyone is innocent. But someone has to clean up the bodies afterwards." Delancey stood up. "Send me that recording. And wipe your nose for God's sake."

"WELL, I OWE YOU CONGRATULATIONS," Director Boleani said, with a wide smile on his round, child-like face. "We just need to wrap it up. The case is over!"

He waited for Delancey to reply. So did Beatrice and Ayser,

who stood at his sides. But Delancey kept quiet, just staring at the walls. Beatrice coughed.

"We still need to find the rest of the bodies," she said.

"This is indeed important. But what's most important is that we have managed to stop these heinous acts and find the perpetrator."

Delancey wanted a hit so badly, but he promised himself today was a clean day. He stared at the diplomas, tokens of gratitude from orphanages and special schools that lined Boleani's wall. Director Boleani lived alone, and maybe that was why he invested himself in social work so much. Delancey felt sweat trickling down his temple. He loosened his tie.

"If we may, sir, we still have some..." he said hesitantly.

"Of course!" Boleani smiled. "I just need you to know how proud I am of you. This was the worst public security crisis in decades. Sleepless hours. Hours of work and dedication from people on the streets and in the offices. It feels good to be over it, Andrew."

"Thank you, sir."

"I plan on giving a presser on Monday. I want you—and Beatrice, of course—to be there with me."

"Thank you, sir."

THE THREE LEFT Boleani's office and walked down the corridor back to their section, talking on the way.

"You will be famous, chief," said Ayser to Delancey.

"No, you," Delancey answered without even slowing his pace.

"Huh?"

"I don't plan on attending the wonderful event. I hope you can relieve me of my duties with the media."

"Me...? Oh, er..."

"You can do it. Now listen, you two." Delancey dragged Ayser and Beatrice to a corner and whispered: "You stop talking with anyone about the case. I'm the only man in the world you give any information to. Understood?"

"What are you ... suggesting?" Beatrice asked.

"I'm suggesting the main suspect hangs himself and writes a fake suicide note while in custody of the most powerful law enforcement organization in the country."

The two agents stared at him. Finally, they nodded. Understood. Delancey patted Ayser on his shoulder.

"Now go, you wanted to be home early."

Ayser sighed, thought of saying something, then just waved his hand and turned to go to the elevators. Delancey turned to Beatrice.

"The IT cyber operations people, they got that email account yet or no?"

"The email account? Andrew, that was some nut. It's not the first time..."

"A nut that knows too many things that happen to be true."

Beatrice sighed. "No, they don't know anything more."

Delancey scoffed. "Cyber operations! Impressive."

They entered their bullpen. It was empty, everyone left for home already. Delancey's stomach winced. He had to take a hit so badly. He stared at Beatrice. They were standing close to each other.

"Agent Lubonsky," he said. "It is an order of the highest priority that you drive me to my place and we spend some time there."

SNOW WHITE PEAKS. Eternal pine trees. Cold wind. And there she comes. The golden-haired girl on skis. Grace incarnate.

Delancey was lying on his back in his bedroom, sweat on his

face, his eyes closed. He could feel Beatrice's head on his chest, her unfurled hair and her warm, naked body pressing against his. He took a deep breath. He tried to remember.

The golden-haired girl ... so long ago he had seen her when he had been with the other kids from the institution on a trip. Some philanthrope had funded the older boys a week in a mountain ski resort. They stayed at a nice, clean hostel, nothing fancy, but for a fifteen-year-old Andrew it was heaven.

Of course he couldn't ski. Their caretaker tried to book the boys some lessons, but after Andrew fell head-first into snow and heard the laughs of the others, he quit. He just stood at the foot of the slope and looked at the long, long carousel of the ski lift and people on skis and snowboards.

And then he saw her. A girl his age, in ski goggles, sun reflecting off her golden hair. She was so agile with her skis, like something out of this world. She passed by him and smiled at him, but he could not muster the nerve to go looking for her later. He knew he had no chance. With his cheap thrift-store winter clothes, his simple outdated hairdo cut by his teacher, he couldn't fight for the attention of a girl like that one.

But the image of her burned into his mind then. It was the image of the world he longed for, one he knew he could never have. Some memories are like anchors cast into the ocean of time, and take one back to foregone years, to other places with so much force, so clearly, that one can almost touch them. For Delancey, such an anchor was the memory of the girl, rapturing him back to the winter break so long ago. Before falling asleep he liked to think about her skiing down the slope so gracefully. It was the best memory he had.

But recently he discovered he couldn't remember it so well. It was getting difficult to invoke those images. They were becoming pale, blurry, and dark. Her face became a featureless blank mask. He couldn't travel back in time anymore. He could feel the memory slipping away from him no matter how desperately he tried. Maybe it was the gruesome case, maybe the drugs. But he felt it was a great loss. As if a part of him had died.

"One more time?" Beatrice murmured, and he opened his eyes.

She was smiling up at him with her head on his chest. It was night, but his bedroom was full of lights from outside, as Beatrice always made him raise the shades. She said she didn't care for making love in a coffin.

"I think I'm done," he answered.

Beatrice was still dreamy from the time he was lying atop of her and making love to her just minutes earlier. She stroked his bruised arm.

"I want to ask you for something."

"Sure."

"Andrew. Stop with this junk. It's killing you."

He sighed and put her hand away. "Thank you for staying with me tonight, Bea."

"My pleasure."

She sat in the bed and fixed her shiny black hair.

"You think Boleani knows about us?" she asked.

"I don't give a damn who knows..." he started saying—and suddenly he stopped. He stared at her with unseeing eyes, struck with some epiphany.

"Andrew?" she said. "What's wrong?"

"Excuse me..." he said and jumped out of bed and started looking for his pants, and when he found them, he started looking for his wallet.

"You're a damn freak, Agent Delancey," she said.

Delancey opened his wallet and took out a dozen cards. On each of them, his email address was crossed out and a new one had been scrawled in his handwriting.

"I changed my email a month ago," he said. "Less than

twenty people know my new email. I'm an idiot. How could I have missed it?"

He sat down at a table and took out a blank piece of paper and a pen.

"Who were the last people I gave my card to?"

"I love you too," she said so quietly he couldn't hear.

12

AT THE END OF THE LINE

While Delancey and Ayser were investigating the body at the docks, Gabriel spent that day at school in a daze. He couldn't stop thinking about what happened in the subway. He stared at the teachers without hearing their words and he thought about the plan for that night.

At eleven p.m., when his mother was fast asleep, he told the demon of her pillow to give her good dreams, and the demon of her cover to keep her warm and cozy. Then he slipped out of their apartment.

The subway line was still closed, the city crews managing the remnants of the accident. He rode on his bike to the night bus stop, got in the back and rode to the last station, where the kidnapper had wanted to get out yesterday.

The strange people on the bus, night workers, drunk punks, and weary women, looked at him with little interest, the hooded teenage boy with his old bent bike, riding the bus across the night city.

The journey to the outskirts was long. Gabriel looked out through the windows at the blocks of flats, those multi-floored galleons of lights passing by majestically. Behind each lit window there was a family, or maybe somebody alone, with their own problems, their own lives. But Gabriel didn't think many of those people talked to demons or looked for children kidnapped by a mysterious, terrifying killer.

Thirty minutes later, the bus stopped by the last station of the subway. Gabriel got off and rode his bicycle to the entrance to the subway. The station was a lonely island of light in a dark, deserted district. He was surrounded with shutdown workshops, with old, outdated advertising banners. It was quiet. A red traffic light moved in the wind. Gabriel heard an owl hoot.

So few people seemed to live here that maybe he had a chance of success turning to the local demons. He asked the demon of the barred and disabled subway escalator about the man in a military jacket and red cap. Then he asked the streetlight.

The demon of the streetlight had seen the man. Said he traveled there often. He showed Gabriel the way, down the narrow alley through which the kidnapper usually arrived or left.

Gabriel got on his bike and rode slowly down the alley. He asked the demon of the alley and the demons of the workshops he passed. Each demon confirmed they saw the man who fit the description. Some had seen the white van as well.

Gabriel hesitated. He remembered the fear. Not when the kidnapper was chasing him down the rushing train—that was pure adrenaline—but the scariest thing had been the still stare of the man's sunglasses, covering half of his scarred face. The memory made Gabriel stop in the dark alley.

"Ombudsman?" Maurice asked softly.

Then Gabriel remembered his little brother. That was more important. He nodded to himself and continued.

The demons of the sidewalk and the mailboxes pointed him down the alley. Its end got lost in darkness, as the line of streetlights ran no further.

Gabriel got a clear feeling the demons were afraid. They answered with reluctance, looking at their feet, eager to hide back in their totems. They were thin and destitute, and there was a shadow in their faces.

But as the demons' fear grew the further he rode down the road, Gabriel actually felt more and more invigorated. His heart beat faster.

"We've got him," he said.

Maurice just looked at Gabriel and smiled without a word, maybe amused with his courage.

The alley had turned into a dirt road, and the pavement turned into black ground, sucking on the tires of his bike, with lumps of cement and quicklime lodged in its oily surface. There were no more streetlights.

They entered the dark zone and Gabriel's heart faltered.

The road led into a forest. There, it became a mossy path, running deep into the darkness between the trees. The leaves murmured and rustled in the night wind. It was quiet.

Gabriel stopped on his bike and looked at Maurice. The demon returned the stare without a word. The boy reached out to the nearest tree.

"Demon of the tree, come out!" he tried in a commanding voice. "I am the Seer and Ombudsman."

Nothing. He pointed at a big, mossy rock by the path.

"Rock, come out!"

Nothing.

"I remember telling you distinctly, " Maurice said in a soft voice. "Works of man. A tree, a rock, anything that lives, is not of your creation. You will not see them and you will not command them. We are lost here."

Gabriel looked around. "No," he said. "You're wrong."

Maurice raised his eyebrows in surprise.

"Oh?"

"The path," Gabriel said. "The path is a work of man."

And before Maurice could reply, Gabriel pointed at the overgrown path under his feet and commanded: "Path! Come out!"

Nothing.

He turned to Maurice, surprised, but before he could say anything, there was a hiss and a moan—and Gabriel saw a naked, skinny man, shivering on the ground on all fours, his skin dirty with black soil, his body covered with scars. His pair of mad eyes glared at Gabriel from behind a veil of greasy hair.

"Go away!" the miserable apparition shrieked. "I am the demon of the path and I am crushed to the ground. Go back! Return!"

"Get a grip on yourself," Gabriel said.

The demon jumped to his bare, bleeding feet, rushed to Gabriel and whispered in his face: "Go back. Or you will meet torture beyond your imagination."

"I will not turn back," Gabriel said, and made the Sign of the Covenant. "I am the Seer and I am the Ombudsman and I'm not turning back. You will listen to me."

The dirty naked man gaped at Gabriel. His bulbous eyes shone in the skull-like, bony face. Then the demon giggled. And then he laughed like a madman.

"You fool," the demon said and disappeared.

Gabriel turned to Maurice. "He's insane," Gabriel said.

"He's been treated in an inhumanly cruel way," Maurice answered. "He will not honor the Covenant. I can't imagine what it takes to make a demon turn insane. We're just too simple for that."

"Come out again!" Gabriel pointed at the path again.

"Go away!" shrieked the voice from the bushes to his left.

"Come out!"

"Go to hell!" yelled the invisible demon of the path, this time from their right.

"Ombudsman," Maurice said quietly. "Let's return to the city and think of a better plan."

"You're afraid?" Gabriel stared into Maurice's yellow eyes. Maurice hesitated, and finally replied, staring at his feet:

"Yes ... for you, Ombudsman," he said plainly.

"So am I," Gabriel said, turned away and started riding deeper and deeper into the dark forest, down the path. Maurice sighed and followed.

After a short ride, they arrived at a point where the path split in two. Gabriel hesitated. Then he chose the right path. They rode on. The vegetation became thicker. Thin branches touched Gabriel's face. And then the path branched again. Gabriel took the left path.

They couldn't see the sky, and it was stuffy in the forest. Gabriel felt like he was in an underground catacombs, with no air to breathe, just silken cobwebs brushing past their faces, and the trees creaking loudly now and again, even though there was no wind.

And then they arrived at another fork.

"We will get lost," Maurice said.

Gabriel took out his phone and opened the map. He saw their position. They were at the beginning of the solid green mass of Shirnev Forest. He zoomed with his fingers and saw only the blue dot of their position, surrounded by a sea of green. There were no paths on the map.

Gabriel switched the view to satellite. He saw a thick mass of trees stretching for miles ... and several places in which the satellite photos were missing. Maurice was right. They were lost here.

Gabriel sighed, put away his phone and started to ride deeper into the forest. Maurice groaned and rolled his eyes before getting on with following the boy.

"I want it to be noted ... this happens against my best minded advice," the demon said. "Ombudsman?"

Gabriel stopped and was staring at something ahead.

"Shhh..." the boy said. "There. Can you see?"

A man-shaped silhouette stood among the trees ahead ... but there was something strange about it. It wasn't human.

At that moment, the strange being saw Gabriel and yelled in a high voice: “Someone’s coming! I notify, I notify, someone’s there!”

Hearing it wasn’t the kidnapper, Gabriel put aside his bike and walked until he could see the person clearly.

It was a demon covered in plush fur, with a round head and a pair of round, hairy ears. His eyes were bloodshot, terrified, and his mouth was missing teeth ... and at its feet there lay a small, dirty, teddy bear.

It was the demon of the teddy bear.

“Someone’s there! A boy! And another demon!” yelled the Teddy Bear. He looked tortured and insane, all shaking.

“Stop screaming,” Gabriel said softly, and made the Sign. “Who are you?”

“I’m a child’s friend, who accompanies her through the hardest nights of fever and fear, to comfort her and bring warmth and calm of heart...” As he spoke, tears flew down the Teddy Bear’s face. “And I failed ... as my owner has been taken to the darkest of all places ... where bad, unspeakable things happened to her.”

“You belonged to a kidnapped child!” Gabriel said.

Just then a big dog's barking echoed in the forest ... and a distant male voice saying something...

“Ombudsman!” Maurice cried in alarm.

A noise of tearing bushes and guttural, low barking exploded in the distance; the dog was storming towards them.

Gabriel leaped up to the teddy bear, grabbed it, stuffed it into his hoodie pocket, and he ran towards the bike he’d left on the path. The twigs whipped him, tearing his skin, leaving lines of blood on his face.

He looked behind him and saw a big muscular beast of a dog, with short light-brown fur, crashing towards him through the forest, barking low as thunder with its black wet maw. And behind it there was a man running, following the dog—the Stellen Street Kidnapper.

"Get him!" wailed the kidnapper to the dog.

"Gabriel, run!" Maurice cried.

And then Gabriel stepped on a gnarled root sticking out from the ground and he fell.

He started to scramble to his feet when he heard the deafening low guttural bark WOOOF just behind him and a heavy, strong body crashed into him and he fell to the ground again.

Gabriel managed to turn around and jammed his left arm into the dog's jaws. The dog bit into his arm and Gabriel felt a terrible pain as the beast's fangs broke through the sleeve of his hoodie and into his flesh. He screamed. The dog's saliva, mixed with his own blood, trickled on his face from his arm, which was the only thing dividing him from the hungry jaws.

"Good boy!" the man laughed from the distance, coming towards them. "Kill the little fucker!"

The dog was big and heavy like an adult man. Gabriel couldn't push it away. Finally, it let go on its own and pushed its muzzle toward Gabriel's throat, ready to bite into the artery. Gabriel's right hand clutched the dog's collar, trying to pull the beast away...

The collar...

"Come out!" Gabriel whispered.

Behind the dog a form appeared, a thin spiky-haired girl with shining eyes and a sadistic smile: the demon of the collar. Gabriel's hold grew weak and the dog went for his throat as in the last moment Gabriel managed to make the Sign of the Covenant with his left hand.

"Tighten up! As much as you can!" he managed to whisper to the demon ... and the dog yelped and Gabriel could see the collar pulling tighter and tighter around the dog's throat, crushing it...

Gabriel kicked the dog off him and jumped to his feet.

The beast was whimpering on the ground, the collar so tight now it couldn't breathe. Its eyes turned whites up, it shuddered for the last time—and it was dead...

Gabriel managed to break out of his paralysis and stormed towards the path. He heard from behind: "No!" as the kidnapper reached his dog and saw what Gabriel had done.

Gabriel jumped on his bike and pedaled as fast as he could, down the path, out of the trees, away from the forest and the killer in it.

"God damn it, what was that?" Giovanni kept asking, floating int the air beside Gabriel storming down the side alleys.

"Just go," Maurice answered in a trembling voice. "We can chitchat later."

When he was sure he wasn't being followed, Gabriel stopped at a bus stop and waited for the night bus to take him back home.

He got on the bus and set out on a long journey back to his apartment, in time to sneak in and go to bed before the screaming flock of seagulls circled his tower block at dawn and before his mother woke at the first rays of sunlight.

13

THE DARK MOTHER

HE WAS BACK HOME at dawn. Hidden in the dark stairwell of his apartment building, between the floors, he whispered fervently to the little teddy bear.

"Tell me everything."

"It's a destroyed house, white and gold, in the middle of the forest. Big, white, many floors, many rooms."

"And the children are there?"

"The bad man keeps them in the basement of the basement. My little owner, my Julia, too. He puts on a mask. And then he does bad things."

The demon of the teddy bear cried and hid his face in his hands. Then he continued:

"I kept company to my Julia. I told her the goodnight tales our Mom used to tell us. I did what I could to give her some hope in this dark, dark place. And now I'm taken away from her and she is lonely and afraid."

"Wait a second..." Maurice said, but Gabriel didn't let him finish.

"Is my brother there?" Gabriel asked in a breaking voice. He felt tears running to his eyes. "Matt. His name is Matt."

"There are many children in the locked rooms below the

house, where one becomes two," the Teddy Bear said. "Many voices and many cries."

"Well, how did you get out of there?" Maurice asked.

The Teddy Bear looked at him. There was a moment of silence.

"Well?" Maurice said, staring at the demon. Eventually, the Teddy Bear just broke out in hysterical sobs.

"I don't know ... I don't remember..." he said.

"That's alright, calm down," Gabriel said. The crying demon slid back into the dirty plush toy and the boy turned to Maurice. "Why are you so tough on him?"

The demon of the playground shrugged. Gabriel picked up the teddy bear in his hands, then checked his phone.

"Mom will be up soon. We have to go home," he said.

Gabriel slipped into his apartment. He took a look in his mother's bedroom. She was still asleep. Yesterday he had told the demons of her sleeping pills—the dozy, fat sisters dressed in many colors—to hold her in their arms and give her good, calm dreams.

He went to his room, left the teddy bear in there, and went to the bathroom. He washed the blood from his hands and put a Band-Aid on the dog bites. Maurice was staring at him in silence, lost in thought.

"We have him now," said Gabriel. "The Teddy Bear will take us to his place. We will save Matt."

"Hm," was all Maurice said in reply.

"Don't worry. I'm going to be more careful this time."

Maurice didn't answer. He was looking at the bathroom door dividing them from the rest of the apartment.

"Something doesn't feel right," he said quietly.

"What?"

Maurice shook his head. He wasn't sure.

Gabriel wiped his face with a towel and crossed the corridor to his room. He stopped in the doorway, surprised.

In his room, by the window, there stood his mother, with her back turned to him, and she was wearing a green military jacket, camo pants, and muddy boots.

"Mom...?" he whispered in awe.

Gabriel's mother turned to him and smiled without saying a word.

"What ... why are you wearing this?" he asked in a faltering voice. He felt dizzy, he felt tingling in his arms and legs, as if he was about to faint. The unspeakable terror made him unable to move.

"Mom. Please ... take it off..."

His mother revealed a long butcher's knife in her hand and she smiled even wider.

"Please..." Gabriel whispered.

His mother jumped at him. He evaded the first blow, but the tip of the knife cut his cheek. His mother giggled and lifted the knife above her head. The rising sun reflected on the blade.

"Come to Mommy, boy!" he heard his mother's voice, full of a monstrous glee.

Crying with terror, Gabriel leaped out of the room and ran down the corridor and looked around in panic. The old closet ... he opened it and hid inside ... it was so tight in there ... he was pressing his back to the rack with different tools, so he grabbed a screwdriver. Clutching it, he stood there in half-darkness shivering and crying without a sound, overtaken with terror.

"Gabriel?" he heard his mother's voice. "What's that, cub? What's going on? Where are you?"

His heart skipped a beat. She was passing by the door to the closet. He stopped breathing and pressed his back against the wall, praying...

Then the door opened.

He cried in surprise.

And pierced the screwdriver deep into his mother's heart.

Only she was wearing her red bathrobe. Not a green jacket.

She gasped, her eyes wide with terror, as if asking, "What have you done?"... and she slid to the floor, the screwdriver lodged between her ribs, slipping out of his hand.

And he saw the second mother, the one in a military jacket, standing there, down the corridor, smiling at him maniacally, with the teddy bear in her hands. Gabriel could only move his lips in a mute shock. The evil mother couldn't stop laughing.

"That was even better than I thought it would be. You killed her! Ha, ha, you killed your own mother!"

Gabriel shook his head, feeling tears streaming down his cheeks.

"Well, you did!" the woman laughed. "Just look at her. Dead as a doornail!"

"No..." Gabriel said and gave in to weeping.

"Did I do well?" the demon of the teddy bear asked the evil mother. "I took you to him. I whispered to you through the pipes and floorboards and streetlights, so you could follow the naughty boy home. Did I do well?"

"You did well," answered the creature with Gabriel's mother's face, smiling hideously.

"Will you spare my owner, then? The little girl Julia? Will you let her go, like you promised?" begged the Teddy Bear.

"Huh?" The monster feigned surprise.

"You said you will spare Julia ... you said to the others ... if we guard you well..."

"Oh shut up already," the woman said, and tore the toy's head off. Its demon cried out and disappeared. The woman threw the shreds of the plush toy aside, reached to her face ... and lifted it off, and midway it became a white mask, and below the mask was the kidnapper, staring at Gabriel with hate.

"And what about you, little friend?" he hissed. "This is going to be interesting..."

Then there were three loud gunshots behind the front door, and it cracked as the lock broke under a powerful kick from the other side.

The kidnapper dived into Gabriel's room and at the same moment Andrew Delancey, a gun in his hands, stormed into the hallway, looked at the mother's body, cried out in surprise, and aimed his gun at a weeping Gabriel.

"Don't move!" Delancey shouted.

Gabriel couldn't speak. He just stared at Delancey.

"Is there anyone else in here with you?" Delancey asked, still aiming at Gabriel. "Hello?" Turning his head, he yelled into the apartment.

He was answered by a loud explosion of rock music, coming from the TV in the mother's room down the hallway. It was so loud the walls were vibrating.

The door to the room was between them, slightly ajar.

Delancey shuddered. He licked his lips nervously, in unbearable tension, switching his aim from Gabriel to the door. Step after step, he approached it slowly, carefully.

And down in the hallway, behind him, the kidnapper darted out of Gabriel's room and ran out of the apartment, unheard in the cacophony of the rock concert. Gabriel was still speechless with his constricted throat; he could only point at the front door and stutter helplessly:

"Thut ... thut ... thut..."

Delancey noticed that and turned immediately to the front door, but it was too late.

"What?" Delancey cried to Gabriel. "What's there?"

And it wasn't even fifteen seconds when two cops ran in through the front door, breathing heavily, guns in their hands. Delancey looked at them with relief; he was waiting for them.

"Agent?"

"Took you some time! Check out the rooms!" He shouted over the noise.

The cops disappeared down the hallway. After a while, one of them turned off the TV and it was silent again ... except for a strange and painful, wordless sound coming from a paralyzed Gabriel's mouth.

"Nobody here!" yelled the cop from the mother's room.

Delancey approached the mother's body, knelt and checked for pulse on her neck.

"Goddamnit, boy," he said. "What have you done?"

IT WAS RAINING the morning when the cops brought Gabriel downstairs, handcuffs on his wrists, his face pale white, his eyes staring without comprehension. As the cops led him out into the yard, he saw two demons of police sirens, thin and dog-like, hunched on the roof of the police cruiser and wailing in the rain.

All around the yard there were neighbors and passers-by looking at him in bewilderment. Maurice followed him.

"Careful, Ombudsman. You want to be really careful now," whispered the demon of the city playground, but Gabriel paid him no attention.

He was looking at an ambulance, its back door open wide, and then he saw paramedics carrying a stretcher, and somebody was on the stretcher, but he couldn't see who that was, as the person had been covered with a blanket from head to toe.

"Who's that?" whispered Gabriel.

"Well, it's your momma, boy," Delancey said and put his hand on Gabriel's shoulder. "Come on, get into the car."

"Just don't tell them anything, Ombudsman," Maurice kept whispering. "Or you'll never see the light of day again."

The cops carefully put Gabriel in the back seat of their car and turned to Delancey.

"Take him to NBI. I don't give a damn what your rules say," Delancey said. "We have detention cells there too."

The cops looked at each other, unsure. Delancey leaned into their faces.

"You don't want to disobey an NBI agent, pals. Not if your families still enjoy your salaries. Okay?"

Delancey crossed the street to his old Mercedes, got in and followed the cruiser with Gabriel inside. The ambulance also drove away, in sudden silence, its sirens switched off.

The onlookers began to disperse. Only one person lingered a bit longer in the rain. Somebody in a green military jacket, muddy boots, with a dog's collar and a white mask in his hand. He was smiling. He didn't like to get bored. He liked games and fun. And that morning was full of them.

Gabriel was sitting in the police car, staring quietly at the ambulance in the other lane. As they passed the intersection, he saw the ambulance turn left.

"Wait, no!" he cried suddenly. "You lost them!"

"Huh?"

"They turned left!"

The cops chortled.

"Go back!" Gabriel said.

"Ah, shut up, you crazy ... you mental shitstain," the cop said.

"Come out!" Gabriel said to someone they couldn't see.

"Shut up I said," the cop repeated.

"Follow the ambulance!" Gabriel said to someone, and with his cuffed hand he made the Sign of the Covenant.

"Yes, Ombudsman!" answered the Police Car, and it made a U-turn at full speed, with screeching tires, and the policemen screamed in surprise: "What are you doing! Hold the wheel!"

"I am!"

"Oh my God!"

They swerved and crashed into a sedan coming from the

opposite direction. There was a terrible noise and quake and the car stopped.

"Holy shit!" yelled the cop. "You alright, man?"

The other cop was bleeding from his forehead.

Delancey, who pulled over when he saw the accident, ran up through the pouring rain to the police car.

"What the hell are you doing?" he shouted.

The cops didn't know what to reply. Delancey opened the rear door and looked at Gabriel.

"You're fine?"

Gabriel didn't answer. Delancey looked back to the confused cops.

"I'm taking him with me. Get out, little fella."

Gabriel stared at him coldly.

"I want to go to my mother."

Delancey shook his head. "Your mother is dead, pal. You killed her."

He grabbed Gabriel by the sleeve, pulled him out of the cruiser, and led him to his Mercedes.

DELANCEY PUT Gabriel on the second floor, in the better detention cells. They looked like humble studios a lonely bachelor might live in: a couch, wallpaper with depictions of nature, a selection of holy books in the drawer of a nightstand beside a narrow, hard couch that doubled as a bed.

Gabriel sat on the coach and stared at the floor.

"I'll make them get you something to eat," Delancey said.

Gabriel didn't answer. He hadn't said a word since Delancey took him into his car.

"You sure you don't want to speak with me about what happened there?" Delancey asked softly. No answer. He hesitated. As much as he wanted to interrogate Gabriel, the law stated that underage detainees had to be interviewed by a child psychologist first. "I'll get someone to help you make yourself at home."

As Delancey was standing in the metal-strengthened door, ready to leave, he heard Gabriel speak:

"I have to go to school."

"Oh yeah?" Delancey stopped and turned to the boy. "You do?"

"I will lose the stipend otherwise," replied Gabriel quietly.

Delancey scowled.

"That will be the least of your worries, sonny," he said, and left the cell.

14

LIKE RATS IN A LABYRINTH

GABRIEL DIDN'T SAY a word for twenty-seven hours. The government psychologist couldn't make him speak either. The boy appeared to be awake all that time, just sitting there and staring ahead, as if his brain was switched off. He drank some of the orange juice they left for him on the table by the couch, but he didn't touch the sandwiches.

Delancey was in the cafeteria ordering his lunch. He settled for a bacon and egg bagel, hold the mayo, when Beatrice called him on the phone.

"He's talking," she said.

Delancey tossed the bagel aside and ran straight to the detention wing. Beatrice was sitting in the surveillance room, facing a large wall screen. On the screen, there was Gabriel, staring straight ahead with that same disabled expression.

"What is—?" Delancey started, but Beatrice silenced him with a raised hand.

"Hush!"

And then Gabriel spoke.

"I have to," he said.

Delancey blinked and leaned in closer to the screen. There was nobody else in the cell with the boy.

"Is he talking to himself?" he asked.

Beatrice shrugged. "Beats me."

"They will do what to me?" asked Gabriel. He listened for the response, then nodded. "Oh, that. Yes, you keep telling me that. Do you prefer I go there alone? After the forest?" Again, silence was the only answer, but Gabriel nodded. "Everything. I can't help my mother now ... but we still can save Matt. Why should I be quiet?" He listened to the answer, then looked straight into the surveillance camera. The impression of Gabriel seeing him was so strong that Delancey made a step back. "Yes, I've seen the cameras. I don't care anymore."

Delancey rushed out of the room.

"Wait!" Beatrice called, but he didn't even slow down.

GABRIEL CALMLY LOOKED at Delancey as he entered the cell. He didn't appear to be surprised. They looked at each other for a second. A manic, scrawny agent in a white shirt and a somber boy in a hoodie, with big dark sad eyes staring from underneath a tangle of dirty hair.

"He keeps them in the woods of Shirnev. In a big, white and golden house, in the basement of the basement," Gabriel said, repeating what the Teddy Bear had told him. Maurice hissed, shook his head, and hid inside the leather bracelet while Delancey stared hard at Gabriel.

"Okay," the agent said. "You're the one who wrote me those emails, correct? The Ombudsman."

Gabriel nodded.

"The watchman from the dump wasn't the real killer, correct?"

"That is correct," was the quiet answer.

Delancey bent over the table and got his face close to Gabriel's.

"How do you know all that?"

There was a moment of silence.

"Demons tell me," Gabriel answered finally, hearing Maurice's exasperated cry from his bracelet.

Delancey stepped back and laughed with disappointment.

"You don't believe me, do you?" Gabriel said.

"Did you expect me to?"

"Close your eye," Gabriel whispered, facing the corner of the ceiling.

"What?" Delancey followed his stare to a surveillance camera, then back to Gabriel, who pointed at Delancey's black tie, made a strange gesture with his left hand and said:

"Necktie. Where have you been before you came here?"

"Excuse me?" Delancey said. "I'm supposed to—"

But Gabriel interrupted him: "You were in a room with a big screen, watching me in secret with a woman you sometimes have sex with. Before that, you were at an eatery of sorts. You ordered a bagel..."

Delancey felt cold shivers running up his spine, like back when his colleagues had seen faces of dear ones in the traffic photo. He felt nauseous.

"You ... you..." was all he managed to say.

"Dark," said Gabriel.

The lights went off.

"Light," said Gabriel.

The lights went on.

Delancey didn't even try to say anything.

"Do you believe me now?" Gabriel asked.

Delancey sat down across the table from Gabriel. He kept silent for a while.

"How do you know all that?" he asked finally.

"I told you."

"And the demons killed your mother, too?"

Gabriel's voice faltered: "I killed my mother. By mistake. I thought it was him."

His shoulders shivered and he had to force down a sob that threatened to overwhelm him.

The door opened. Beatrice stood in the corridor, looking unnerved.

"The feed suddenly went off," she said. "What's going on here?"

AYSER, Beatrice and Delancey were standing next to the table opposite Gabriel, who was still sitting on the couch and staring at them. He had just finished telling them what they had been doing that day since morning.

"Well?" Delancey said. "How about it, Agents?"

"It … it will sure take a moment to take all that in," Beatrice said. "I feel like checking into a madhouse. Ayser?"

"I need to sit down," Ayser said in a weak voice.

"Be my guest," said Delancey.

Ayser sat in the chair. "It is a dream," he said.

"Suppose it is." Delancey shrugged. "That doesn't answer what we should do now."

"How did you know the kidnapper was there? In the Wests' apartment?" Beatrice asked Delancey.

"I didn't. I made a list of all the people I gave my new email to. They were the first name on the list and I went there first thing in the morning. I saw our boy here return home from some suspicious expedition. I followed him and I was standing by their front door, thinking of what I should say, when I heard screams. I called the nearest dispatch and came in."

"But you didn't see the kidnapper there?" Beatrice asked.

Delancey shook his head.

"He was there," Gabriel said, and everyone looked at him. "He told the TV to play loud and ran out so you didn't even hear him."

"Or so you say," said Ayser. He was staring hard at the

teenager, then turned to Delancey. "Just one question, chief. The kid's got some weird powers, that we can agree on. But why exactly do you trust him?"

Delancey moved his eyes from Ayser to Gabriel, thinking hard. That was a good question.

"For all we know..." Ayser said and pointed at Gabriel. "You can be the kidnapper. Who just stabbed his mom with a screwdriver."

There was silence.

"I lost my mother and my brother is missing," Gabriel said slowly. "I can make your guns explode. I can make your clothes smother you. With a bit of thinking about the correct method, I can make this whole building collapse. But I am sitting here ... talking to you. That's the only reason to believe me you're going to get."

He stood up. He was shorter than everyone else in the room, but somehow they all took a step back.

"You are afraid of me," Gabriel said. "And I am afraid of him. That's why I'm talking to you. And there is still a chance to save my brother and other children. Help me."

Beatrice nodded to Delancey. Delancey looked at Ayser. Ayser gave him a quick shake of his head.

"We have nothing to lose," Delancey said in reply.

"This is madness," Ayser said.

As they came back into his cell, and Delancey told him what they had decided, Gabriel looked concerned.

"Where?" he asked.

"To the city prison, at Vadomski Street," Delancey said. "I have reasons not to trust our local personnel, so I don't want to leave you here. The prison is high-security and handled by the police, not NBI. You'll get special treatment, a solitary cell in the VIP section. I'll let you know as soon as we have our guy."

"No," Gabriel said, "I have to go with you."

Delancey sighed.

"Listen. I have three dozen SWAT operators with tactical vests and assault weapons. You said yourself that this man has more ... power than you ... more power over objects. He's almost killed you. Now is the time for you to stay low, get some rest, get a grip on yourself, and let grownups handle the job. How about it?"

Something about the easy confidence in the man's voice convinced Gabriel. He nodded.

"Now I need you to be a good boy, on your best behavior. It won't be long. I'll come to you myself after we're done and I will tell you how it went. Deal?"

Gabriel nodded again.

WHEN THEY LEFT Gabriel's room, Beatrice asked Delancey with disbelief: "Boleani gave you the squads?"

"Boleani won't know a thing," Delancey said. "And I have a feeling it's for the better. As far as he's concerned, the deal is over. The mayor congratulated him and now Boleani's unable to admit to his incompetence."

"And...?"

"We're going on our own," Delancey said.

"And we do what? Comb the, what, two hundred acres of forest? It will take forever."

Delancey nodded. "We need to take a closer look. Ayser, could you get us a detailed map? And whatever you can find on the area."

"I've got a feeling we're all going to need therapy once this is over," Beatrice said. "Today I've seen things that are beyond comprehension. I feel as if I was sleepwalking."

Delancey stopped. "Look, I don't think there are demons of things. Come on. I think both the boy and the fucker possess some kind of psychic powers. That is all. We're never going to understand the whole world. We can just try to make the most of what we have here. Like lab rats in a labyrinth."

GABRIEL FELT good when he could give all agency to the matter-of-fact, tough adults of Delancey's squad. He was missing a child's right to just listen, to just do what he was told by someone who knew better.

Maurice was silent on his wrist.

They put a blanket over his shoulders. They put him in an unmarked car and drove him to the prison at Vadomski Street. He saw a tall gray wall, topped with barbed wire, and in the wall there was a big metal gate, painted yellow. The gate opened and they pulled into a narrow yard.

The car was surrounded by cops. They knew Delancey. They opened the door and Gabriel got out and went towards the gloomy building with them. He could feel pairs of eyes looking at him from the barred windows.

"See you soon! Have fun," Delancey called through the open window of his car.

Inside, Gabriel was searched by a stern, tough-limbed woman with short gray hair, while the two cops who brought him here looked on. She took away his phone.

"I'm sorry, dear, but this has to stay with me," she said. "Also, please remove that."

Gabriel looked at his leather bracelet. Maurice didn't show up to protest. Gabriel hadn't seen him since he had told Delancey about the demons.

"Here, let me help you," she said, and reached to untie the leather cord. "The knot is very tight. Do you mind if we cut it? Oh!"

She screamed and moved back, waving her fingers in the air and blowing at them.

"It's hot!" she exclaimed. The cops looked at her and she decided to ignore the strange event.

"Okay, I guess there's no harm in that," she said with a warm smile. "It's too short to be dangerous. And what have you done, dear, to be taken here?"

He turned his blue, empty eyes on her. "I killed my mother," he said.

The woman's smile disappeared. She turned away from Gabriel and began to fill in a report.

They took him to a cell, gave him food and drink. It was quiet on the floor he was on. Gabriel lay down on a bunk bed and closed his eyes. He thought about officer Delancey gathering troops to go into the woods. He thought about the warmth in his mother's arms and a dry cry tore out of his chest.

AYSER PUT his tablet on the desk. Delancey and Beatrice leaned over it. It was a map of Shirnev Forest, with some open area marked in the middle.

"What's there?" Beatrice asked.

Ayser smiled.

"Nothing. But there was supposed to be ... this."

He swiped the screen to reveal a colorful, computer-rendered visualization of a luxurious gated community in the middle of the forest. Children laughed and ran across green lawns, and played in a water park surrounded by trees. Condo buildings, all made of darkened glass, white marble, and golden ornaments, stood in a circle in a panoramic image, while the forest behind them stretched to the horizon in gentle slopes.

"What the hell's that?" Delancey said.

"New Eden. A gated community planned by Rasner Development, a company which is now bankrupt. The CEO put his head into a gas oven amid a taxation scandal which broke out just after they started with the construction. Since then, the land has been in between various hands, in disputed territory."

"It's a scandal the government sold them the land. I mean, it's a national nature reserve, isn't it?" Beatrice said.

Delancey exchanged looks with Ayser and they both smiled at her naivety.

"Money can settle more than you think," Delancey said. "Even with national nature reserves."

"Yep. Until it runs out and you gas yourself," Ayser said, and swiped to a real-life photo of an impressive, super-modern condo building, looking like a shiny white slab against the sky.

"They managed to finish one of these before the shit hit the fan. It was supposed to be the model for investors before they carried on with constructing the rest. Been there for twelve years. There was nobody to bulldoze that thing because, well, who's going to pay for that, right? So, hell knows what's going on there now."

Ayser and Beatrice stared at Delancey.

"Well? What do you think, chief?"

Delancey nodded.

"Get the word to Ruslan's boys. We're moving there at first light."

"If that's the place..." Beatrice started, "if that's the place, there are children in there, scared and ... being tortured maybe even as we speak. Any moment we sit here just prolongs their suffering. Don't you want to go there now?"

Delancey sighed and shook his head.

"I'm afraid to go there now, Beatrice. We need Ruslan. They won't be ready before dawn, at the earliest. And we need light. It's an unknown area. We need to see well."

Beatrice pursed her lips.

"Best time for action," Ayser told her softly. "The manual's 101."

Eventually, she nodded.

"Let's do this," she said.

15

NEW EDEN

THE FIRST GRAY light was shining above the mangled spidery treetops of Shirnev Forest when three large BearCat vehicles moved down the highway that ran along the forest's edge. They turned onto a simple asphalt road with crumbling edges, taking them deeper and deeper into the woods.

Ruslan was sitting in the car of the first van with Delancey. Tree branches swiped along the windshield. Ruslan opened a bottle of sparkling water with a loud hiss and offered it to Delancey. Delancey shook his head.

"Don't like sparkling water? Helps me fill my stomach when I'm intermittent fasting," Ruslan said, taking a big gulp. He pointed at the road. "How the hell did they manage to transport the whole construction crew there, cranes and all?"

"Twelve years ago, Ruslan. Plenty of time for the road to grow over," Delancey said.

They passed by some huge old pipes lying alongside the road, and some slabs of cement.

"Whoa!" Ruslan said. "Seems the trip's over."

There was a tremendous mass of tangled metal on the road ahead, impossible to go around it. It looked like thick, steel reinforcement bars, mangled and rusting, thrown on a pile by a giant, barring further way into the forest.

"Well, seem we're walking from now on," Delancey said.

He was the first one to get out of the car. He jumped to the cracked asphalt from the high step and looked around.

"Kill the engines!" he said.

The three drivers obliged. He saw Ayser and Beatrice get out of their van as well. He turned to the forest and listened.

Now the engines weren't running, you could tell how silent the forest was. It was too silent. You could expect at least some rustle of leaves, some whisper of the wind, a bird's song. But here ... nothing. Delancey swallowed with unease. He felt suffocated.

He nodded at Ruslan, who then barked a command into his walkie-talkie. The SWAT officers began getting out of the vans. They looked like armadillos with their gray and thick tactical vests and helmets.

Delancey walked around the barricade and stopped in surprise.

"Well, I never," he said.

Ayser and Beatrice joined him to look at what he was staring at. There was a toy, a plush elephant, sitting in the middle of the crumbling road. Its bright blue, plush fur was stained with dark spots.

Delancey made a few steps ahead and crouched in front of the toy. He looked at its round, plastic eyes.

"Agent!" Ruslan called.

Delancey stood up. Ruslan was pointing at something in the bushes, several feet away from the road. Delancey went there, pushing through the thorny bushes that scraped his arms.

In the forest, on the mossy, wet ground, there was a little pink ballet shoe. A snail was making its slow, torturous way across the shiny, lacquered surface, leaving behind a glistening and sticky after-path.

"What do you make of it?" Beatrice asked.

Delancey stood up and without a word went back to the road. He picked up the toy elephant and stuffed it into the pocket of his jacket.

"Spread out," he called to the SWAT agents. "We're moving towards New Eden in a wide formation. Go deep into these woods. Let me know whenever you find something."

Delancey, Ayser, and Beatrice walked down the dilapidated road while the SWAT agents moved through the forest.

It wasn't even five minutes until Delancey's radio crackled and he got a report of the first found item. Then came more, one after another. Things belonging to missing children, strewn across the forest. A toy car. A naked doll. A pacifier. As they were moving closer and closer to the old construction site, the agents found over twenty toys, socks, shoes, hats, all belonging to children. It seemed as if the ground zero, the spot of the New Eden development, was in the middle of a spiral composed of missing children's belongings, spread out in huge circles across the forest.

Delancey told them to leave the things where they found them. After one more report, he stopped walking and turned to his colleagues.

"Spies," he said in a sudden realization.

"What?" Ayser asked.

"I remembered the teddy bear the West kid told me about. Those toys are spies. It's a net of spies for the kidnapper. If what that boy says is true..."

"I don't think we should be talking about that ... if you want to keep this job," Beatrice noted quietly.

But they both knew that if he was right, the kidnapper already knew about their arrival.

They were walking for an hour.

Delancey felt it in his bones. Years spent on the streets had fine-tuned his survival instinct and he knew the feeling. They were being observed. The demons of the items belonging to lost kids were watching them and forwarding the news of their arrival, mouth to mouth, all the way up to the kidnapper, sitting in the middle of this web of forlorn objects, like a scheming, malicious spider.

Delancey had long suspected that the investigation of the Stellen Street Kidnapper would be his end, that he would not make it through this case alive. He had come to terms with that knowledge. And yet, right now, there was nothing he wanted more than to be out of these woods, in the open, away from the gnarled, black trees, the humorless gray clouds hanging low above them, the suffocating stiffness, and the horrid things they were finding in the moss.

THEY CAME out of the woods into the construction site. It was razed clean of trees, an empty, overgrown space with deep trenches and rebar sticking out of the ground, impotently rusting, aiming into the sky. In the middle of the site there stood a tall, foreboding building. Its walls of white marble had turned black with soot from vagrants' fires, its windows all smashed, golden finishings torn and broken.

The agents came out of the forest and stood there and stared in wonder at the site.

It was quiet.

Ruslan made a gesture and his men rushed along the wall of the forest, surrounding the area in a wide circle, so nobody could escape.

Delancey's eyes scanned the empty windows, the gaping holes for doors, whatever parts of the inside he could see through the holes. The white building was still, and at the same time scarier than anything he'd ever experienced in his life.

He put in an earpiece.

"Everyone can hear me?" he asked.

Ruslan and his SWAT team leaders came in one by one. *Affirmative.*

"We're closing in," Delancey said. "Pay attention to all signs of movement. We don't know where the kids are, so there's no time to waste. We can be seen now. So let's move fast before the bastard gets some ideas."

"Understood," he heard Ruslan's answer in his earpiece.

"Alright. Move!"

The agents started running towards the building, aiming their guns at the windows, at the doors. When they were twenty feet away, they could smell how it stank. Of something rotting. Of old cabbage gone bad.

Ten feet.

"No signs of life," said Ruslan over the radio.

And then, a terrible deafening digital shriek exploded in their ears, a scream that penetrated every inch of their heads. The SWAT operators threw themselves on the ground, grabbing their helmets in agony from the sound coming from their earphones.

Delancey screamed as the explosion of noise pierced his eardrum. He tore out the earpiece and threw it on the ground. Still holding his ear, and gritting his teeth from pain, he saw Ayser's and Beatrice's mouths moving as they were asking what had happened, but he couldn't hear them.

He picked up his gun he had dropped when the noise had struck and he ran towards the door to the building. Ayser and Beatrice followed him, while the SWAT officers were still ripping their helmets off, grown men crying from the pain in their ears.

DELANCEY BARGED INTO THE LOBBY, kicking the door open, and looked around frantically, aiming left and right. The lobby was bare, full of concrete rubble, lit skimpily with sunlight coming through the cracks and holes.

There was a collapsed concierge desk. There were gaping holes of elevator shafts. They saw a broken door in one of the walls, and behind it there were stairs leading down to the basement.

The first SWAT officers, their heads bare, were entering the lobby. Some of them, still deafened and with damaged ears, stayed outside. Delancey nodded at Ruslan and moved towards the staircase to the basement.

"Wait!" Ruslan said. "Let my men..."

Delancey just looked at him and continued. Ayser and Beatrice joined him.

"That's against protocol!" protested Ruslan. "You don't even have a vest..."

They ran down the stairs. After several steps, Ayser turned on his flashlight, as the sunlight had no way of reaching them. Delancey strengthened his grip on his gun. He could feel his own heartbeat, the blood pumping through his veins, pulsating in his temples.

They ran down the stairs, the circle of light from Ayser's flashlight moving along the walls. White tiny particles of dust danced in the ray.

And then they saw them.

Three dark silhouettes at the feet of the stairs, with guns and flashlights.

"Wait!" Delancey hissed. "It's a mirror."

A large wall mirror was built into the wall opposite the stairs.

"Who puts a mirror in a basement?" Beatrice whispered.

Delancey took the flashlight from Ayser and shone it to the right.

There was a long corridor with doorways on both sides, and it opened at the end into a large space.

"Andrew!" he heard Ruslan's voice calling him from above. "Andrew, come back here!"

He sneaked to the first doorway. Shone his light inside. Some rubble. An old, dented bathtub.

Next room down the corridor: broken, long planks in a heap on the concrete floor, "WELCOME TO PARADISE," written with something dark on the wall.

Next room, empty. Next room, empty.

"Andrew!" Ruslan's voice was coming from the distance.

"What the fuck does he want?" Ayser whispered.

The rooms were empty.

They arrived at the entrance to the large room at the end of the corridor. It was a huge, open space, with columns holding up the bare ceiling.

"What's that?" Ayser said.

"It's a garage," Delancey said. "For the people who were supposed to live here."

There were no missing children.

They heard a terrible grating sound and reached for their guns. Sunlight filled the garage. The heavy, tall metal doors fell to the floor with a loud din. Ruslan's men had broken down the driveway doors with their crowbars.

Delancey walked up to them and saw Ruslan standing in the sunlight with a stern face.

"We have to go, Andrew," Ruslan said, and showed him his phone.

"What?"

"Boleani called. Angry as hell."

"He's back?" Beatrice asked.

"Apparently. And apparently you haven't consulted this deployment with him."

Delancey kept quiet. Then he spoke through his gritted teeth: "Your men will go back into this building, Ruslan, and search it from top to bottom. Understood?"

Ruslan looked at him for a while.

"No, I don't think so, Andrew," he said finally, shaking his head. "It's not your money buying bread for my family. I'm not risking it. And I'm not making my men risk it."

Delancey's phone started ringing. He checked the screen. Boleani. He cursed and declined the call.

"Ruslan, can't you see? We're at the verge of solving this case!"

Ruslan smiled at him sadly. "Sorry."

He turned and walked up the driveway.

"Come on, boys!" Ruslan yelled. "We're going home."

Delancey turned to his colleagues. Ayser's and Beatrice's phones were ringing. They weren't answering, looking at Delancey in anticipation.

"Well? What are you waiting for?" snapped Delancey, and walked back inside.

IT TOOK them ten hours to check every room of the condo building. From the basement to the rafters. The units didn't even have floorboards. There were no panes in windows. It was empty.

Their cellphones kept ringing throughout the day.

They went outside at sunset and looked at each other in the golden light of the setting sun. They were tired.

Delancey took out his phone with "Boleani calling" displayed on the screen. He picked up.

"Sorry, boss," he said to the phone. "I missed your calls."

16

LIKE A SCREAMING METEOR

TWO HOURS LATER, Delancey was standing in Boleani's office staring into the angry eyes of his boss.

"I made them stay with me," he said about Ayser and Beatrice. "It's not their fault."

"Spare me that talk. You're so arrogant to think that you have any impact on the consequences for my employees."

Delancey lowered his head and looked at the carpet. He wondered who was the snitch that had informed Boleani. Ruslan? Ruslan's men? They were just grunts following orders. Beatrice? Ayser? Impossible.

"There was no time," he said finally. "We got a solid lead. We found the place where the children are being kept."

"Oh you did?" Boleani raised his eyebrows. "And where are they?"

Delancey didn't answer. After a while, he took out the toy elephant out of his jacket and showed it to his boss.

"The forest is full of those. All around the New Eden development. Toys, clothes..."

"Yes, people throw trash into the woods. As one of the benefactors of Save The Planet, I think I know that better than you do," Boleani said.

"They belong to the missing children," Delancey interrupted. "We need to pick them up and show them to the parents..."

"Oh, we will. Or we won't, if I decide there is no need to drag depressed people through more pain just because one of my employees has decided it is him running the whole show."

"Sir, I'm not—"

"You move a whole team of armed operators, using government vehicles, on their working hours, to investigate an old, empty building in the middle of the forest, spending taxpayers' money and peddling false hope to the families of missing children. Forgive me the affront, Agent Delancey. But if I may ask, as the last time I heard I was the director of this institution, what exactly was the evidence of the children being there? Why did you go there of all places? Is the stress of the work getting to you finally? Are you losing it?"

Delancey stood there in silence. He felt a drop of sweat roll down his cheek.

"Sir, the West boy..."

"The West boy! A poor sap who lost his mind after his brother got kidnapped and who stabbed his own mother. Did you ask him how he knows all that?"

"I—"

"No, you did not! The Stellen Street Kidnapper is dead. He hanged himself. He drowned his victims in the old port. It is only because of the incompetence of those idiot divers that we didn't find more of them. Probably taken by the swell. What we need is more divers, not losing our time and money scouting the forest for bear shit."

There was silence for a while. Boleani changed his expression and examined Delancey carefully through his shiny round glasses.

"So far, I have ignored your ... weaknesses, Agent," he said in a new, quiet tone. "I've done that in light of your achievements.

But today you made me wonder whether your habits aren't taking a toll on your ability to perform ... and whether they do not influence the clarity of your mind. I feel for you, what with what the media gossiping about your past, but you're compromising your position, and that of the whole bureau."

Delancey didn't understand. "Media, sir?"

Boleani looked surprised. "You don't know?" he asked.

Delancey shook his head.

"Oh..." Boleani lowered his head, as if embarrassed. "Sorry. The ... tabloids are running pieces about ... the circumstances of your childhood."

Delancey just stared at him in disbelief. Boleani opened a website on his laptop.

"*The Herald*," he read from the screen. "'Brother of his own mother. Who is the man running the most high-profile case in the country?' *The Inquirer*. 'Tragic childhood secrets.' *The Belldog Times*. 'Son of the Monster and his Grandson in One.'"

Boleani closed the browser. "I'm sorry, Andrew," he said. "It's filth. I will be filing for defamation and obstruction of investigation. But you know what they say. Media, the third power. They do what they want. I think it's better you have a few days off. I will give you as much time as you want. Fully paid, of course. Don't let it get to you."

If Boleani had thought Delancey would explode at the news, he was in for a disappointment. The short, ugly agent was just standing there and staring at him, his face inscrutable.

"Can I go, sir?" Delancey asked finally.

"Dismissed."

Delancey moved to pick up the toy elephant from Boleani's desk, but his boss stopped him with his outstretched hand.

"That's it, Agent."

Delancey nodded and went out of the office, closing the door behind him. Boleani sat there for a while, staring at the elephant. Then, he turned to the wall of his office and he said:

"He will take his drugs now."

Someone in the wall giggled in response.

DELANCEY STOOD in the hallway of NBI headquarters, while a few miles away, in the prison, Gabriel stood by his cell door. They both held their phones at their ears. A guard watched Gabriel as the boy listened to Delancey tell him about the ill-fated and senseless trip to the woods.

"I'm calling like I promised," Delancey said. "Here's Delancey. Remember me?"

"Yes," Gabriel said. "Have you found him?"

"We didn't find anyone," Delancey said. "There was a building and the building was empty. I'm calling like I promised. Now I have to go. I'll call you once I decide what to do next."

Delancey disconnected. Gabriel stood by his cell door, staring at the floor, the dead phone at his ear.

"Is it over?" the guard asked, meaning the call. "You're done?"

Gabriel didn't answer.

"Hey! Give me back that phone. The call's over!"

Gabriel nodded, handed the phone back to the guard, and moved to his bunk bed.

IT WAS dark in his office. Delancey kneeled by his desk and unlocked the top drawer. Only he had the key. Inside was his black metal lunchbox. The sight of it alone was enough for his famished body to shiver in expectation.

He had no time to waste.

He took out a vial, punctured it with the needle and let the syringe drink up the contents. With shaking hands, he shot Atroposine up his vein and sighed in relief ... and he felt something was wrong at the very moment.

Terrible pain in his chest, pushing out all air.

Nausea, like his whole body wanted to vomit itself.

He was dying the most hideous-feeling death he could imagine. The light grew dim and he fell.

MEANWHILE, thousands of feet above the clouds, on flight A28 from Los Maines to Basel, two pilots were struggling with the controls. The air hostesses smiled at the anxious passengers and told them everything was alright. Behind their fake smiles they were afraid too. And the pilots were afraid and sweating under their elegant black caps. The airplane had changed its course 180 degrees and wasn't reacting to manual controls. It was just flying somewhere else. It appeared ... it was flying back to the city.

"Mayday, mayday!" repeated Jorgen Schwarz into the radio. But no communication was coming in or out from their plane. His copilot, Arlo Bederer, took off his cap and began to pray silently, his tears falling on his shirt and trousers.

The demon of the plane, unseen to them, was standing behind them, his face frozen in sorrow and determination. He had to follow the orders whispered to him by the man in a green military jacket and dirty boots back when they were still on the ground, refueling. The man had walked up to the plane on the airfield, unobstructed by the crews. He'd made the Sign of the Covenant. And the Airplane had to listen to the man, for he was an Ombudsman.

The plane tilted and the city below filled their fields of vision. Jorgen held the yoke and pulled so hard toward himself that his fingers were white and he screamed. The second pilot covered his eyes and screamed, too.

Much like the rest of the plane. Everyone was screaming. Bags and tablets and cups and inflight meals flew across the cabin as the plane took a nosedive, gaining speed, crashing through the layers of clouds and then towards Los Maines, down, down, like a screaming meteor.

The pilots closed their eyes.

The demon of the plane stood there, solemn and intense, staring at the exact point where he was steering.

The city prison on Vadomski Street.

"OMBUDSMAN."

Gabriel opened his eyes on his bunk and stared at Maurice, who was standing by the bars of his cell and looking out into the corridor. He seemed agitated.

"Gabriel."

"Yes?" Gabriel asked quietly.

"There's something wrong," Maurice said.

Gabriel sat up on his bunk.

But before he had a chance to answer, the speakers in the corridor and the speaker in his cell all crackled and a male voice filled the air.

"Hello, little friend," the speakers said in unison, and Gabriel felt weak and all blood rushed from his face as he recognized the voice.

There was a murmur coming from the other cells as the inmates reacted to the strange voice.

"I've found out who you are, Gabe my friend," the Stellen Street Kidnapper laughed. "So you're little Matt's brother, eh?"

"No..." Gabriel whispered in panic. "No!"

"I must say, your curious nose led you into trouble," the man continued. "Or rather, it brought trouble on little Matt. You see, I thought I could spare him before..."

"Please..." Gabriel said, shaking his head.

"I don't know how you've gained my power. But that's not important now. I'm many times stronger," the speakers boomed in unison. "You're a worm compared to me, like the rest of the humans. But you've still managed to irritate me a little. You killed my dog. You've caused me a slight discomfort. So I thought, maybe little Matt should pay for your sins."

There were running footsteps in the corridors and surprised voices of policemen.

"Who's that? Who's speaking?" someone asked.

"I have no idea, there's nobody at the mic," came the answer.

"Ombudsman, don't listen to him," Maurice warned. "Tell the speakers to shut down."

But Gabriel didn't pay attention. He stared at the speaker in his cell, pale and terrified.

"Let me tell you what I did," continued the voice sweetly.

"No!" Maurice cried.

"I told him what you did to your own mother," said the voice and chortled. "I told it to him in detail. In very vivid detail."

Maurice looked at Gabriel, to see how he would react. Gabriel sat there, staring at the floor. His head low.

"And then ... I killed him," continued the terrible voice, and the kidnapper smacked his lips. "He died with the thought of you killing your mother. He wasn't happy."

Gabriel felt his heart breaking.

"And I'd like you to think about that in your last moments. Goodbye, little fucker."

Then the walls shattered and a powerful explosion tore everything apart as the airplane falling from the sky crashed straight into the prison. The gust of hot air pushed Gabriel against the wall. He hit his head, and everything went black.

He opened his eyes. He could only hear the din in his ears, and saw the world in flames. The wall was broken, the ruins of the ceiling were on the floor. Fires were raging on the floor above.

He wanted this to be the end. His mother was gone. Matt was gone. There was no point in any more struggle. Let the fire consume him.

Maurice hovered above him, saying something. Gabriel tried to turn his head away.

"Stand up!" yelled Maurice over the roar of the flames.

There was so much power and desperation in the demons' voice that Gabriel obliged.

And then something strange happened. Maurice outstretched his hand toward Gabriel. And Gabriel took his hand and he could feel it, even though Maurice was an immaterial demon.

Gabriel followed Maurice out of the cell, stepping through the collapsed bars.

The fire was raging everywhere. But Gabriel realized he didn't feel the heat. Maybe from the shock. He saw his clothes smoking as he followed the fast-walking demon of the playground through the collapsed corridor.

The dust in the air looked like fiery red fog. They passed broken, charred bodies, walked over severed body parts, scraps of blackened flesh and boiling puddles of blood.

Gabriel leaned in half in an attack of coughing from smoke in his lungs, but Maurice urged him on.

In the ruins of the dining hall he saw the nose of the airplane, two dead faces of its pilots flattened on the windshield.

There was fire everywhere, and the demons of burning objects stood around them howling to the sky in painful death. Some of them recognized the Ombudsman in Gabriel and stretched their hands to him, begging for help.

On the other side of the prison, a strange figure entered the blazing corridors. A man in a golden fireproof suit, his head in a fireproof helmet. He smiled as he walked down the rubble, dragging behind him an empty collar on a leash.

"He's here!" Maurice exclaimed. "Quick!"

He dragged Gabriel towards a wall of fire. Gabriel stopped, terrified of the flames. An open inferno was blazing right in front of him.

"You will be alright!" Maurice bellowed. "Close your eyes. And run!"

"But—"

"RUN!"

Gabriel closed his eyes and ran into the wall of flames. He felt a breeze of open air and he tumbled and rolled down the concrete rubble, tearing the skin on his arms. As he ran out of the smoke, he saw the streets in chaos, people running and crying around the burning ruins of the city prison and the scattered remains of the exploded airliner.

He ran through the streets, screaming, bleeding and desperate. What he went through pushed him away from being a human.

Meanwhile, in the inferno, the killer in the fireproof suit reached Gabriel's cell and walked in, dragging the collar behind him.

"I will do to you what you did to my dog," he said, his voice muffled in the fireproof helmet, mixing with his heavy breath. "You know how long I had to train it? I had to sic it at many little kids. All this to waste. Poor animal."

And the cruel smile on his face died as he saw there was no trace of Gabriel.

"No!" he cried and whipped the wall with the leash in fury. Then he turned to the dying demons of burning things and yelled: "Where is he? Where is the fucking boy?"

MAURICE LED Gabriel through the streets, crossing the district into the industrial port. They ran against the stream of curious, alarmed people swarming towards the epicenter of the catastrophe.

Maurice seemed to have an idea of where they should go. Breathing hard, Gabriel found himself on the bank of the river coming from the bay.

Maurice shuddered and pointed at the river.

"Look, Ombudsman, I don't love water, as I believe I have already said. There is a small island over there, in the middle. See it? I will get back into the bracelet and you will swim there. You can swim, can't you?"

Gabriel just stared at him.

"Listen. We can't trust anything. The sidewalk under your feet, the old newspaper carried by the wind, every thing will betray you and bring the news to him. Only in the wild will you be free of his spies. Now go!"

Gabriel nodded and jumped into the dirty, cold water. He swam towards the small island covered with thin, leafless trees and thorny bushes.

As he covered the half of the way he realized he could end it right now. The water was cold and dark and welcoming. It offered him peace and forgetfulness. The end of pain, the end of struggle. He closed his eyes and stopped swimming and let the water swallow him, embrace him. He was going down, deeper and deeper, free at last, when a terrible scream exploded in his head:

"Swim, Ombudsman!" bellowed Maurice in the middle of his brain.

His body retched from a paroxysm of even more suffering, and he swam to the surface and reached the island.

In wet clothes, he shuffled his feet deeper into the tiny piece of land. It was no larger than twenty feet in diameter. He walked into the bushes and fell facedown into the skimpy, pale grass. The wail of sirens and the roar of special forces helicopters above the city center was quiet here, distant.

Maurice appeared next to him. "Call out the demons of your clothes," he said. "Swear them to secrecy. Order them not to tell anyone you are here. Let them not talk to any object floating by on water or carried by the wind."

But Gabriel wasn't answering, bereft of strength, lying face down in the grass, not moving, not thinking, his eyes closed, taken over by a lifeless stupor. He wished for nothing more than a rest without end, the cease of all pain and worry.

"Ombudsman?"

He yearned for nonexistence, and in his head, behind closed eyes, he kept falling, falling, falling into darkness.

"Gabriel?"

There was no reply. The demon of the playground sat on a stone and stared at the unconscious boy with his yellow, mysterious eyes, which seemed eternal.

It was getting dark.

17

REBORN

TWO DAYS PASSED, and Delancey knew no time.

He suffered in darkness that sucked all will to live. He had never felt so bad in his life. In rare moments of consciousness, when he was returning to the surface of his tiresome slumber, he heard a steady beep of some machinery, or footsteps, or a familiar voice—only for a wave of convulsions to come and sweep him back into the depths of malignant suffering.

In the sweaty, hopeless visions, he suddenly felt a cold breeze on his fevered brow and he saw the snowy mountain slope; he was a boy again, on the trip to the mountains. He saw the golden-haired girl go down the slope on her skis and he almost cried out in surprise and joy. The vision was real as never before—he was there.

The steady, calm wind blew off the snow from the pine trees that lined the mountaintops. Delancey was standing at the foot of the slope and she was coming down towards him and she turned as she slowed—the small fountains of snow erupted from under her skis—and he felt a long-forgotten wave of longing as she approached him. He couldn't move and just stood there and stared as she stopped next to him. She was smiling at the glum, skinny teenager he was again, with her full pink lips, and Delancey felt that he was returning the smile too. She reached up to the goggles covering her eyes, and combing back the mass of her hair she lifted them, revealing her black eye sockets swarming with white worms.

Delancey screamed in his hospital bed.

Ayser looked at Beatrice with worry. They were sitting by Delancey's bed in the central military hospital. Delancey grabbed Beatrice's hand and squeezed it so hard she hissed from pain. He opened his eyes and looked at them like a maniac.

"Kill me," he whispered, and his head fell back to the pillow wet with his sweat.

The door opened and a nurse entered with a tray of glass vials.

"Visiting hours are over," she said. "You have to go."

Ayser nodded and they stood up.

"No," Delancey moaned.

"It's the first time we've heard him talking since we brought him here," Beatrice said. "I think he's getting better."

"I'm no doctor and I can't discuss our patients," the nurse said. She filled her syringe with the contents of one vial. "Now, if you excuse me..."

"No!" Delancey's face contorted as if he was a small child about to start crying.

The nurse emptied her syringe into the IV bag over Delancey's bed. The substance from the vial mixed with the transparent contents of the bag flowing through the catheter into Delancey's veins.

Delancey felt another hit of putrid smell and nausea. His heart clenched itself like a fist on a stone and he fell back into the infinity of suffering, back into the thousand restless deaths.

"Good night, chief," Ayser said. "Gonna see you tomorrow."

The nurse looked on as Ayser and Beatrice left the hospital room.

. . .

Night had fallen. The river whispered quietly. Over the hum of the wind there came sounds of a distant party on a brightly-lit ship, dance music and echoes of happy cries of people having fun. The officials were still in shock and the city was still half-paralyzed after the plane crash, but that didn't seem to affect people's need to party.

Gabriel sat in the middle of the small island on the dirty river that divided the city in half. He was staring at the thin, sick trees, stones, sickly pale grass, and black, oily earth. Nature still lived alongside the technology of men—forgotten, weak, mutated, but he couldn't command it.

He stood up rapidly. Surprised, Maurice looked at Gabriel as he walked to the river's edge and stared at the city, lit with thousands of windows. Behind each window there was an apartment, and people who lived their lives, their loves and their hurt.

"Even if he didn't lie…" Gabriel said quietly.

"What?" Maurice asked. He stood up and walked up next to Gabriel.

"Even if Matt really is dead," Gabriel said, "the kidnapper is still out there. Even if I can't help Matt anymore, I can make sure he doesn't hurt anybody again."

Gabriel couldn't see it, but Maurice smiled in response. The boy reached out to the distant party ship floating by in the distance.

"You!" he yelled.

"What are you doing?" asked Maurice, surprised.

"What do you want?!" called the demon of the ship from the distance. "I'm carrying the night of fun and drink and free love on my shoulders. What do you want, oh strange, lonely boy, standing on a desolate dirty island?"

"I want you to come here and take me to the other bank," Gabriel said.

. . .

THE CREW of the party ship could never explain why their ship disobeyed all steering maneuvers and turned ninety degrees, to float up to the small island, where a strange boy in a dirty hoodie climbed aboard. The young, partying people greeted him with surprise and inebriated cries of joy. Everything new that happened made them happy that night. The ship's crew looked on, unsure if they were sober themselves. Perhaps they were dizzy and hallucinating from all the smoke of hashish hanging over the deck.

The boy pushed through the dancing crowd to the buffet table and started eating the finger sandwiches and shrimps as if he hadn't eaten for weeks, while the ship turned again and went to the bank, despite the helmsman's desperate yanks at the steering wheel.

GABRIEL GOT off the boat at the Western Pier. The boulevard was alive with lights and full of people, enjoying their early night drinks. He pushed to Kosciusko Street. It was quieter there, in the shade of centennial elms, and approached a rundown, empty cab.

He gestured to the cab's demon.

"Clients are here. Open up."

He got into the back seat, Maurice beside him.

"Do you know of any shops with electronics open at this hour?"

"There's a large general store at Bender Alleyway. Twenty-four seven," grunted the demon behind the wheel.

"Let's go there, then."

The cab started with screeching wheels and dashed down the street. Maurice looked at Gabriel with a curious smile.

"We're going shopping?"

"We're going shopping for guards and scouts," Gabriel answered. "It was the last time he will ever surprise me."

The driverless cab moved through the night streets until it pulled over next to a store.

"That'll be fifteen dollars," the demon said.

Gabriel smiled.

"Please wait for us here."

THE STORE WAS BRIGHTLY LIT, but there were very few people inside. Bland background music was playing. Gabriel hid his face in the hood, found security cameras and told them to be quiet about what they were about to see.

They walked down to the electronics aisle. There, Gabriel took two simple smartphones and two startup sim card kits.

"Is the second one for me?" Maurice asked.

Gabriel ignored him and threw the phones into the basket. Then he approached the section with drones. He picked a universal drone charging pad by Hikosaki and lots of batteries. Then he scanned the exhibited drones and approached the biggest one.

"Come out," he said.

The demon of the drone was a small but energetic old Japanese man in a pilot's cap, with round goggles and sporting a short gray beard. He bowed to Gabriel.

"I am Captain Nakamura, ace of the skies! My Unmanned Aerial Vehicle Hatsuka MKII is capable of the longest range and fly time in this whole store. Can I help you?"

Gabriel returned the bow.

"Honored to meet you," he said. "Listen, Captain Nakamura..."

. . .

After exchanging a few words with Captain Nakamura and showing him the Sign of the Covenant, Gabriel had a walk through the aisles with TVs, fridges, and automatic vacuum cleaners to the section with backpacks and chose a large and sturdy one. He opened it, put the charging station and phones inside, and casually approached the sensor gates. A large security guard was standing there, flirting with a blonde cashier.

"Didn't you forget to pay, boy?" he asked.

Gabriel turned to the inside of the store and said calmly:

"Now."

A loud buzz filled the store and a gust of wind swept around odd papers as the drones lifted off one after another from their exhibition places and moved through the air towards the exit, led by captain Nakamura.

"Stop! What's going on?!" cried the guard, running through the store and jumping, attempting to catch the escaping drones.

The sensor gates flashed red and buzzed the alarm as Gabriel was walking out of the shop with the squadron of drones flying all around him, buzzing in the air.

Behind him, the security guard and the cashier were chasing automated vacuum cleaners dashing all around the floors and crashing into displays.

Gabriel jumped into the cab and told it to drive several avenues downtown, next to Maines City Park. He stuck his head out the window and watched the formation of drones in the night sky, following the cab dutifully. Satisfied they weren't being chased, he told the cab to open its trunk and watched as the drones swept down from the sky into the trunk, landing one after another, without the cab even stopping.

"Good job, Captain Nakamura!" Gabriel called.

"My life is my duty!" answered the pilot from the trunk. It was clear he was pleased with his exploits as well.

Maurice laughed. "This is the perfect show. You have my attention," the demon said.

Gabriel ignored him. He turned to the demon of the cab.

"Next stop … NBI office. Next to Demianov Square."

"Next stop?" said the cabbie. "We're not finishing there?"

"We're never finishing," Gabriel answered, looking out the window. "Until it's done."

18

THE NIGHT VISITOR

DELANCEY OPENED HIS EYES. There was a huge pain in his head, and he felt ready to throw up. Nausea was his most common friend these days.

Through the pulsating heat in his temples, he looked at the ceiling of his hospital room. There was the shadow of light from the glass window separating his room from the hospital corridor. A night in a hospital is different from anywhere else. It is enormous, full of waiting and readiness. The labyrinth of corridors extended far into the innards of the night. He had been here long enough to know those sounds by heart. The steady sound of heart monitors, the fast footsteps of a nurse hurrying to a patient requesting assistance, the squeak of bed wheels on the linoleum floors, the frightened voice of an old man asking if he is dying. All in the distance, all through the walls, all muffled.

Delancey moaned and closed his eyes. He was feeling so hot. The pillow was soaked with his sweat. And yet he had no strength to lift his hands and turn it to the other side.

Suddenly, he noticed that it got quieter than usual in the corridor. He heard footsteps. Careful, light footsteps were getting closer and closer to his room. Somehow Delancey knew the person was coming for him.

They're about to finish me off, he thought in panic. With all his strength he tried to move his arms and legs to get off his bed and to hide. But his own body was too weak. He clenched his jaw in desperation.

The footsteps stopped and a shadow appeared on the floor. Delancey couldn't even lift his head to see. Waves of nausea pulsated through his head.

The shadow stood there for a while and then approached his bed.

A cold, small hand touched Delancey's head and pushed it back to the pillow. His vision was floating, but he managed to see a silhouette in a hooded jacket.

"Do you recognize me, Agent Delancey?"

He tried to see, but his eyes burned and teared, so he had to close them.

"It's me. Gabriel."

Delancey opened his eyes again. The boy looked like a shadow of his old self, thin, pale, dirty and bruised, with blood and dirt sticking to his hair. A walking dead, devoid of hope, devoid of light.

Gabriel looked at the drip in Delancey's arm. Then he looked at the IV bag.

"Chemical. Show yourself."

The boy stared at the small, twisted, giggling demon of the chemical substance in Delancey's drip.

"They're giving it to you so you don't ever get well," Gabriel said to Delancey, and pulled the IV out of the agent's wrist. There was bleeding from the hole in his hand. Gabriel took gauze from the bedside cabinet and tied it around Delancey's wrist.

"I guess it'll be some time before the effect wears off..." Gabriel said, and sat on Delancey's bed. "Can you talk? Can you tell me what happened?"

Delancey curled in a torsion and felt vomit boil up in his

throat, strangling him, suffocating him. Gabriel quickly reached over and moved Delancey over the edge of the bed. Delancey vomited bile on the floor, pain tearing his stomach apart. Gabriel looked at that without emotion.

"The stairs to your office building at Demianov Square saw you being carried down on a stretcher to an ambulance," Gabriel said. "And now it seems your hospital care leaves much to be desired. Somebody wants you silent, Agent Delancey."

Delancey was holding to his bed, wheezing.

"Do you have anybody left?" Gabriel asked him. "This man and woman who worked with you? What are their names?"

"Raymond Ayser ... Beatrice Lubonsky," Delancey whispered.

Gabriel nodded and took out his new smartphone.

"Find the numbers to Ray Ayser and Beatrice Lubonsky," he ordered two demons, the demon of the phone and the demon of its sim card. "Call them and tell them to be here as soon as they can."

He put the phone back into his pocket and turned to Delancey.

"Well, Agent Delancey," he said. "It's time to go."

He put Delancey's arm over his neck and lifted him. It was good the adult man was short and emaciated so that Gabriel could bear his weight.

"I reached Beatrice Lubonsky," the demon of his phone said. "She said she's coming. Raymond Ayser doesn't answer."

"Thank you."

They staggered up to the door to the corridor and Delancey hesitated.

"Don't worry," Gabriel said. "The cameras are looking the other way."

In the brightly-lit corridor, the doorknob to the nurse station rattled as a nurse on the other side kept yanking on it and knocking on the door, but she couldn't get out, and the communication lines were shut down.

Gabriel dragged Delancey down the corridor and they took a turn. There was a policeman on the floor, crying silently, bent over his boots with shoelaces drawn so tight he couldn't walk, the bones in his feet cracking under the pressure.

"What is happening?" whispered the policeman. "It hurts ... it hurts..."

"I believe this is a man left here to guard you, Agent Delancey," said Gabriel, dragging Delancey on. "I had to modify his shoes a little, as you can see. And I had to relieve him of this," Gabriel patted a police-issued gun in his pocket.

The demon of the elevator opened the door as soon as he saw them.

"Please come in, gentlemen," the demon said.

Before stepping into the elevator, Gabriel turned his head to the policeman on the floor.

"Laces, let go," he said.

The automatic door closed behind them as the policeman cried from relief.

Beatrice stopped her car with a screech of tires at the public entrance to the hospital. She saw the door open and Gabriel carrying out the weak Delancey.

As they went out, the glass door closed behind them. Two orderlies ran up to the door, chasing them, and started banging on it as Gabriel dragged Delancey towards the parking lot.

"Here!" cried Beatrice and jumped out of her car to help.

They put Delancey in the back seat. Gabriel sat in the front.

"Go!" he yelled.

Beatrice stepped on the gas pedal and darted out of the hospital lot. They passed by Gabriel's cab parked by the curb. Gabriel leaned out the window.

"Follow us!" he said and the cab's lights turned on by themselves and the cab got moving, following Beatrice's car.

"What's going on?" she cried. Gabriel was looking out the window as they were speeding down a street. "Where are we going?"

Gabriel finally looked at her and she saw his changed eyes, like black holes.

"I don't know yet," he said.

The car shuddered, and Beatrice cried out as someone rammed into them. She managed to pull the car out of it and looked in the rearview mirror.

A sedan was chasing them.

Gabriel looked behind.

"Who's that?" Beatrice asked.

Gabriel shrugged. "A car."

"What?"

She searched with her eyes in the rearview mirror to see the who was driving the sedan. There was nobody there.

"Go in circles! We need to lose them first!" Gabriel cried.

"Them?!"

Beatrice gasped and turned the wheel, their car missing a yellow school bus coming from a side street by inches.

Nobody was driving the bus.

"He's learned I'm back," Gabriel said. "He's turning the city against me."

They sped down the street, followed by the school bus and sedan, crashing into the barriers and trashcans. The bus veered and a rain of sparks exploded from its side as it brushed against a wall.

"He's told cars to attack me when they see me."

"Pull over! I repeat, pull over!" a crackling voice from a loudspeaker blared and they heard a wail of the police siren. A night patrol had discovered them and was following.

Gabriel stuck his head out the side window. The wind was

howling by his ears, blowing his hood and his hair, as he made the Sign of the Covenant and yelled to the cars:

"I am the Ombudsman! You will listen to me!" he was shouting over the whizz of the wind and roar of the engines.

"You will die!" yelled the demons of the sedan and the school bus in unison, crunched on their cars' roofs. "You are the one he told us about! To find you, to kill you!"

"How many of you are there? How many cars he's told to find me?"

"We are thousands!"

He heard a gunshot and a bullet grazed the roof of their car. A policeman leaning out the window of the cruiser was aiming at them.

"The police have orders to shoot us on sight," said Gabriel. "So not only demons are against us."

He reached out his left hand, with his fingers making the Sign.

"This is the Sign of the Covenant!" he yelled to the demons. "Go and find your master. And tell him ... I'm coming for him!"

The sedan and the school bus swerved and their tires squealed as they stopped and made a U-turn.

Just then, Beatrice cried and they heard a gunshot and she grabbed her left arm. Blood trickled between her fingers. The policeman had shot her through the door.

"You!" Gabriel cried to the demon of the police car. "Stop!"

The police car stopped abruptly. The policemen's heads bobbed forward as their seatbelts caught them.

"Help me!" said Beatrice, holding her shoulder, driving with one hand. "God, it hurts..."

"Come out, demon of the car," Gabriel said.

The demon of Beatrice's car was a man with a mullet and mustache, wearing a leather jacket.

"Drive straight on, be fast, but careful," Gabriel said.

“What’s happening?” Beatrice cried as the car gained in speed and she felt she no longer controlled the steering wheel.

“Relax,” Gabriel said. “Let the car drive.”

Beatrice lifted her hands off the wheel and watched in awe as the car moved down the street with agility and smoothness, like a trout in a stream.

“You can take care of your wound now,” Gabriel said. She saw him turn rightwards to someone invisible and ask: “Where do you think we should go, Maurice?” He listened to the answer and nodded. “Yes. I mean, he’s just one man. He needs to do everything in person. He can’t make one car command another car to do his bidding, or something like that. He’s not all-seeing. And he’s not all-powerful.”

“Who are you talking to?” Beatrice asked.

Gabriel didn’t answer. He shifted his gaze to another invisible being and said:

“Listen, Car, there’s a motel I saw once just outside the city, on Jerusalem Avenue.”

They all leaned to the side as the car took a sharp turn.

“Be fast,” Gabriel said. “We can’t risk any more of his things noticing us.”

Beatrice’s phone rang, but she was still in pain and unable to take it out of her jacket pocket.

“Who is calling, Phone?” Gabriel asked.

“It’s Raymond Ayser.”

19

REST

The motel was called The Queen of the Highway. It stood at the outskirts of the city, a mile off the LM-2 Freeway. A concrete square of a parking lot with offices and owner's lodging squatting on the side. A two-floored L shaped building for the guests, each room having an individual entrance from the gallery.

Beyond the city borders was just a sandy wasteland stretching for miles. The gaudy neon sign with the motel's name shone against the blanching sky above distant hills.

Ayser lived on that side of Los Maines, so he arrived long before them. As Beatrice's car and the cab pulled into the parking lot, he was already waiting, standing next to his rugged 4x4 SUV with worry on his innocent face.

He watched as Beatrice and Gabriel got out of the car. The air was chilly at the end of the night. He nodded at them without unnecessary questions.

"I got us a room," he said, and showed them a keycard in his hand.

Then he noticed the cab pulling up next to them and saw there was nobody inside. He cursed and shook his head.

"I was hoping we were going to stop with the demons," he said in a weak voice.

Gabriel looked around and found a CCTV camera attached to the eaves of the motel's first floor.

"Don't look," he said quietly to the camera, making the Sign. Then he looked back at Ayser. "Help us carry him."

They opened the back door. Delancey was asleep. At least he seemed asleep.

Ayser grabbed him under his arms and pulled him out of the car. As Beatrice couldn't help because of her wounded arm, Gabriel grabbed Delancey's legs. His bare feet were long and pale, with blue veins visible under the skin. He was still in his hospital robe.

"Damn, I didn't think," Ayser said. "I'm an idiot. Our room is on the second floor. We need to go up the stairs."

"Quick!" Gabriel said. "Before someone sees us."

Ayser marveled at how light his boss was, even with his medium height and frail frame. He carried his limp body in his hands, looking at the black hair sticking to his forehead, which was glistening with sweat.

They carried Delancey upstairs with Beatrice helping them as much as she could. They put him on a narrow bed in the dark, modest room, and covered him with a blanket. He was shivering. Gabriel closed the heavy, dusty curtains and turned on a lamp on a nightstand.

"Fix me up," Beatrice said to Ayser and she sat on a dingy sofa. She undid the buttons and Ayser helped her take off the blouse. She remained in her bra. Her left arm and shoulder was smeared with blood.

Ayser brought a wet towel from the bathroom, sat next to her and began to clean the wound. Beatrice hissed.

"Easy," he said. "It just grazed you. There's no bullet."

"Are you sure? Hurts like hell."

"I'll be back soon," Gabriel said and went outside.

. . .

Gabriel went downstairs to the parking lot and took a deep breath of cold air. It was welcome after the musky stuffiness of their room. He stood under the yellow lamps on the concrete lot, a small teenager with his face covered with a hood. He walked from lamp to lamp, trashcan to trashcan, car to car. He swore all demons around to secrecy. The demons promised him to say no word of their staying here at the Queen of the Highway.

Maurice stood beside him, mysterious and grinning. Gabriel turned to him.

"Do you think they'll listen and protect us? Or am I just wasting my time?"

Maurice shrugged.

"You're an Ombudsman. They will listen ... until someone more powerful comes along."

"I've managed to change the orders he gave to the cars that were chasing us. Doesn't that mean I'm more powerful?"

"Only when he's not there."

Gabriel smiled an unhappy smile.

"I understand."

He looked around. It was dawn. The surrounding wasteland stretched for miles, under the sky crossed with contrails.

He looked to the small shimmering lights on the horizon—the city skyline. Then he heard a noise and looked back at the motel. Ayser and Beatrice were coming down the stairs.

"We need to go," Ayser said. "I have to calm down my family."

"And I need to have someone more skilled check out my arm," Beatrice said. "We can come around five, after work. We don't want anybody to connect us with Andrew's disappearance..."

Gabriel nodded. "Bring him some clothes," he said. "And his gun, if you can get hold of it."

Beatrice hesitated. She exchanged glances with Ayser.

"Gabriel, we ... what exactly do you want to do now?"

Gabriel looked her in the eyes.

"I want to find and kill the fucker," he said, and he didn't sound like a teenager anymore. Maurice smiled behind him, but neither Beatrice nor Ayser could see the demon.

"Please don't go yet, we need to settle something," Gabriel said.

Gabriel went to an ATM next to the motel's entrance, told its camera to look the other way and asked the ATM for two hundred dollars. Then, Beatrice went with the money to the sleepy motel owner, showed him her badge and asked him to not interfere with the federal operations center they'd set up in one of the rooms.

After they drove away in Ayser's car, Gabriel started carrying the drones from the cab into their room. He thanked the demon and told it to go back to the city and keep its mouth shut about what had happened here.

"You owe me forty-nine dollars, not even counting the tip!" protested the demon of the cab.

"It's on you tonight. Get lost."

Gabriel went back to the room and locked the door. With electrical tape, he attached his second phone to the biggest drone. He connected a drone charger to the socket and opened the window. He told the drones what to do.

When he finished with that, he lay down on the sofa and stared at the ceiling. He was thinking about his mother. He clenched his jaw and his eyes.

MAURICE WOKE him up with a quiet, "Ombudsman..."

Gabriel jerked awake from the dreamless sleep on the sofa. Maurice stood above him and gestured towards the bed. Gabriel looked.

Delancey was sitting up in his bed, wrapped in the blanket and shivering. He looked at Gabriel, stood up and staggered to the bathroom. Gabriel heard vomiting. Then running water. Delancey was washing his face. He came back into the room, his hair wet, and he sat in a chair. Keeping balance was still difficult for him.

Gabriel sat up on the sofa.

Delancey nodded at him.

"What's up?" he said.

"It's good to see you alive," Gabriel replied.

"Likewise, I guess. Where are we?"

"In a motel outside town."

Delancey nodded again. "You escaped from the prison?" he asked Gabriel.

"I escaped from the burning and exploding prison, to be precise."

"What?"

"He brought down a plane into the prison to kill me. But he failed."

"He blew up Vadomski Penitentiary? With a plane?" Delancey shook his head. "I take a nap for a few hours and see what happens..."

"I hid on an island where he couldn't find me," Gabriel said. "And then I decided to find you. It wasn't difficult. I asked the stairs to your building if they saw you. And they said that you were carried outside and put into an ambulance. The only thing left to discover was which hospital they took you to."

There was a sudden loud buzz and Delancey jerked in surprise. A drone flew in through the back window and hung in the air, the wind from its rotors blowing in their faces. The second drone, which was standing on a charger, turned on its engine, hovered into the air and flew out the window, while the first one lowered itself onto the charger.

"Security," Gabriel explained to Delancey.

Delancey was silent for a while.

"Somebody messed ... with a medicine I take," he said eventually. He felt a rising wave of nausea coming over him at the memory. He stood up and ran to the bathroom to vomit again.

After all was done and he was breathing hard over the toilet, drops of sweat dripping from his forehead, he realized that he was never going to take Atroposine again. His whole body reacted with revulsion to the mere thought of putting it back into his system. He didn't know what to make of that, not yet.

He drank some water from the tap and came back to Gabriel, who was opening the curtains. The sunlight illuminated the inside of the modest motel room. Delancey squinted and moved his chair into the shadow.

"At the hospital, they were lacing the drip you were connected to as well," Gabriel said. "So you couldn't wake up."

Delancey stared at Gabriel. After the death of the teenager's mother, there seemed to be no feeling left in him. He spoke in strict down-to-earth words, in a calm, quiet voice. But there must have been unimaginable heartbreak under that façade. Delancey wondered how the boy was able to carry his burden.

Delancey watched Gabriel move his head slightly as he was listening to one of the unseen demons, then the boy nodded and turned back to Delancey.

"By the way you were guarded by the police, it seems that somebody in your circle wasn't keen on us stopping the real kidnapper, don't you think?"

Delancey kept quiet for a while, then he gestured at his hospital gown and said, "I need to get some clothes. And then I need to go and have a talk with Boleani."

"No."

"Listen, kid, it seems you saved my life. Thank you. But I did the same for you beforehand, so there's no debt here, right? And you're not in charge here."

"Those children are still alive," Gabriel interrupted and Delancey stopped speaking. "We need to get to them first."

"We don't know where he keeps them."

"We do. You've been there."

"New Eden? That ruin in the forest? It's completely empty! We searched it for hours..."

"Have you checked the basement?"

"Of course."

"The basement of the basement?"

"What?"

"The toy bear I found in the woods said '...in the basement of the basement.' I told you."

"What does that even mean?"

"It means there must be a basement below the basement."

"It was just one floor! Empty rooms, a garage. No other stairs or..."

Delancey grew quiet under Gabriel's stare.

"Then we need to find it," Gabriel said.

His phone rang. Gabriel answered and listened for a while.

"Thank you, Captain Nakamura," he said, and scowled.

"What's wrong?" Delancey asked.

"It's the leader of my drone scouts. Says a car is coming."

Gabriel turned on the loudspeaker.

"Try and see who's inside," he told Captain Nakamura.

They waited in tension until the demon replied, "The man and woman who were here last night."

"Your friends are coming," Gabriel told Delancey. "Beatrice and Raymond."

"Wait a moment, that was the voice of a demon? Of a drone? Demons can call you on the phone now?"

Gabriel shrugged. "A phone speaker is an electronic device. All devices are controlled by their demons. A demon makes the speaker emit sounds. So I don't know why you're surprised."

"So, I can tell a demon to call me on the phone and I can hear it, like you do?"

"I don't think you can tell a demon to do anything—no offense," Gabriel answered. He stood up and unlocked the door.

He watched as Beatrice and Ayser pulled into the lot and they quickly ran upstairs to their room. Ayser almost screamed with joy at the sight of the conscious Delancey. He grabbed him in his arms so tightly Delancey gasped for air. They'd brought his change of clothes from the office.

"I believe this is yours," Beatrice said, and threw his gun and NBI badge on the table.

"You're the best, Bea. How did you get that?"

"Let's just hope they don't watch the surveillance from the repository anytime soon," she answered.

Delancey weighed the gun in his hand, already thinking of a good use.

"And a special order..." Beatrice fished in her bag and took out two big paper bags with a Don Pechuga logo.

Delancey unwrapped a cheeseburger from his favorite joint and smelled it in delight.

"You're perfect."

They ate the burgers and drank soda from paper cups.

"What's going on at the office? Is Boleani there?" Delancey asked. The feeling of warm food in his stomach did him good. Not to mention the taste of his favorite cheeseburger and sweet cola.

"It was empty. Most people were in the field, I guess," Beatrice said. "No trace of Boleani. Do you think he—?"

"We have to suspect everyone at this point," Delancey said. "Who poisoned me? Who set up the van at the pier, just one day after we learned about it from Gabriel? And who set up my very alternative therapy at the hospital? As far as we're concerned, the bureau is compromised at this point."

Nobody answered. When they finished eating, they sat down to work out the plan.

"We're going back to New Eden," Delancey said to his colleagues, and exchanged glances with Gabriel. "It is possible the perpetrator will be there. This time we can't tell anyone."

"Why?"

"Because they will stop us."

Silence.

Beatrice shook her head.

"I can't believe this shit."

"Our enemy can command objects," Gabriel suddenly said, standing up. "We need weapons which are simple and without mechanisms. Knives which are not spring knives. Clubs. He is mortal, so you can shoot him, but you would need to be very fast or act from concealment, so he has no chance to interfere with your weapon. That's why the simpler, the better. Now regarding clothes. Nothing with a belt or laces. No regulated bracelets or necklaces. Nothing he can tamper with and incapacitate you. Be prepared that he can have a gun, but I think I can stop it ... I hope."

Gabriel took a deep breath. "He can look like another person. Someone you know, someone you love..."

"He has this mask," Delancey added. "He was wearing it in the photo from the traffic camera. That's why you were seeing people you knew, and the program saw no face at all."

Ayser seemed embarrassed at the memory and looked away.

"It's ridiculous. What good does such a mask do, even if it existed?" Beatrice said. "What, I see my beloved uncle who's in a different country at the moment, and I'm going to be hella surprised! It's not exactly a way to hide in the crowd. Why would he need such a mask?"

"To kidnap children," Delancey answered.

There was a second of silence, then Gabriel stood up.

"The only thing that is safe when fighting him is another human ally," he said. "He can command things, but not people. That's what I understood on the island. That's why I turned to you for help. Get more people you can trust."

The agents looked at each other.

"Ruslan?..." Ayser said.

Delancey shook his head. “He’s Boleani’s most trusted man. I doubt he will listen to us. As we could see, catching the real kidnapper hasn’t been exactly Boleani’s number one priority. Calling Ruslan would be suicide.”

“So it’s only us?” Beatrice asked.

“Well, who else? Volunteers from the internet? The victims’ parents? We can’t drag civilians into that without knowing what awaits them.”

“I have an idea for a weapon that is not mechanical and can act on far distances,” Gabriel said. Everybody looked at him in sudden silence. “We need dogs.”

20

THE ROAD INTO DARKNESS

AT ELEVEN P.M. Ayser showed up with two K9 Unit German shepherds in the back seat of his car. He had borrowed the dogs from his brother-in-law, who worked at the Central Police Station. He rolled down his window and looked at Beatrice and Gabriel waiting for him in the motel's parking lot.

"Goddamn fleabags! My backseat is hairy like a mongrel," he said without much joy.

"Ah, look at those good boys!" Beatrice cried.

Gabriel packed his drones into the trunk of Beatrice's car. Delancey walked out of the motel and approached them. Beatrice looked at him closely.

"Still a bit pale, chief," she said.

"That's the look I'm going for this season," he answered. "I'm feeling golden."

He didn't tell them that he still felt weak and got dizzy when he stood up too rapidly. He walked up to Ayser's car and leaned through the driver's window. One of the dogs growled.

"Easy there, boy," he calmed the dog, and turned to Ayser, grim behind the steering wheel. "Wow, your car finally smells of something else than you." Ayser half-grinned in response. "I wanted to ask you ... do you still have some of your dad's medicine?"

"Sure."

Ayser reached into the glove compartment and handed Delancey the metal hip flask.

"Thanks."

Delancey stepped away from the car and took a good sip of whisky and shivered with pleasure as hot energy spread throughout his body. He looked at Gabriel and Beatrice standing by her car.

"Well, the Nut Squad is complete. What are we waiting for?" he said.

THEY DROVE around the city from the east, through the side streets to evade the cars searching for Gabriel. For a long time they were driving next to train tracks and humongous, bland warehouses.

Beatrice turned on some electronic dance music on the stereo, but the mood in the car remained somber.

Gabriel took out the gun he had in the pocket of his hoodie. It was the gun he had taken from the policeman at the hospital where Delancey had been kept. He called out its demon. It was a thin woman with an evil smile wearing a leather jacket, her eyes twinkling with mischief.

"What's your name?" Gabriel asked.

"I'm Alissa, Ombudsman. I'm the world's most trusted police pistol. I was growing bored and feeling useless in the service of my previous owner. I yearn for blood. Got any wet jobs for me?" she hissed.

"How many rounds do you have?"

"My magazine's full. I've got fifteen seeds of death, ready to be planted."

Gabriel nodded. “I’ve never shot a gun, so I expect you to help me.”

“Just point me at the miscreant and whisper: *Kill!* And I will take care of the rest,” Alissa said.

Beatrice and Delancey only heard Gabriel. They exchanged glances, both thinking about how otherworldly their situation was, driving to the lair of a killer and kidnapper led by a thin teenager who kept talking to invisible spirits.

THEY PASSED by the subway station at the end of line C-17, where Gabriel had walked in search of the kidnapper what felt like so long ago now. He had been a different man back then, he thought, while staring at the halogen lamps surrounding the escalator to the underground station.

They drove on for another mile and arrived at the turn into the forest road.

“Pull over,” said Gabriel.

They waited in the car as Gabriel walked a few steps to the road and ordered it to be quiet. The demon of the forest road was a proud woman in hunting clothes.

Gabriel came back and they took the turn and drove down the forest road. The moon was almost full, a waning gibbous, and it was the only source of light there, painting the tops of the pines silver. Beatrice, who was leading the two-car convoy, turned on the high beams. Sharp rays of light illuminated the mossy trunks of the trees on both sides of the road. Delancey felt like he was going down a waving and turning intestine of some hideous monster.

No animal showed itself during the whole of the way into the mysterious forest.

They arrived at the rebar roadblock and killed the engines. They got out of their cars and stared at each other in the moonlight in silence. The only sound was the hum of the wind and a distant calling of a night bird they didn't know.

"Let's get cracking with unpacking," Delancey said, breaking the spell and opening the trunk of Beatrice's car. He removed his belt and holster, putting the gun behind his back in his waistband. He took one of two baseball bats, handed it to Beatrice and grabbed the other one.

"What do you have?" he asked Ayser.

Ayser flashed a knife.

"It's a real military dagger," he said. "No spring mechanism, like you said," he looked at Gabriel and made a testing slash in the air with satisfaction.

"Better take my bat," Delancey said.

Ayser looked at him, surprised.

"You're holding the knife wrong," Delancey said. "Are the spaces between the ribs horizontal or vertical? When you hit that way, you're going to stop on a rib and never reach heart or lungs."

Ayser was silent for a while. "Yeah, I'd better take the bat."

They exchanged weapons. Delancey slid the knife into the holster and then into his pocket.

Ayser released the German shepherds from his car and held their leashes in one hand. They sniffed the air loudly, excited beyond measure, city dogs surrounded by unknown smells of nature.

"Hold it!" he hissed, and yanked on the leash as they tried to pull him into the forest.

Gabriel put on the backpack with Captain Nakamura's drone. He could feel his gun heavy in the pocket of his hoodie. He turned to the agents.

"We go through the forest," he said. "Fewer eyes."

They walked into the deep forest. The black trees were moving in the wind. They turned on their flashlights.

“There’s no trace of toys,” Delancey said. “Do you know anything about that?”

Beatrice shook her head.

“Someone picked them up,” Delancey said. “Before we could show them to the parents.”

They thought about Director Boleani and grew silent. It was an unpleasant thought. Even more so in the big unknown they were approaching.

Ayser touched Delancey's arm. “Andrew,” he said quietly. “About that stuff the media said about you ... you know, the childhood thing, about your mother and father...”

Delancey tensed. He didn't answer. He just nodded.

“I'd like you to know that doesn't change anything in my eyes,” Ayser said. “I, well, I admire you, and think you're the best damn boss we were lucky to get.”

Delancey nodded and patted the young agent on the shoulder. “I don't think it's the best time for this namby-pamby, Agent. But thank you.”

Gabriel noticed that Maurice had come out of his totem and was moving beside him, silent and somber.

“Are you scared?” Gabriel asked him. Maurice just smiled. “Because I’m not. I don’t feel anything anymore.”

“If so, you’re the most powerful person here, Ombudsman,” Maurice said. “I would hate to lose you.”

Gabriel looked at him, surprised, but suddenly Delancey said: “We’re here,” and Maurice disappeared.

Gabriel stopped them. They were standing on the edge of the forest, looking at the deserted construction site of New Eden. The ruined building rose in the center of the clearing like a single rotting tooth.

Gabriel put the drone on the ground.

“Be fast and quiet, Captain,” he whispered. “Go high so nobody sees you and see what you can see.”

Captain Nakamura nodded, soared up and maneuvered

among the tree branches into the open sky. Then he moved over New Eden.

Gabriel's phone vibrated. It was Nakamura.

"All clear, all quiet," Nakamura said. "No signs of life."

Gabriel turned to the agents.

"Wait here," he whispered.

He walked briskly to the edge of the forest and stood before the construction site. Captain Nakamura was circling the sky high above him.

"Everyone, come out," Gabriel said.

The site was populated with demons of the ruined foundations and construction tools. A skinny, famished crowd, staring at Gabriel with bewildered, mad eyes.

"Hush. Not a word from you," Gabriel said to them and made the Sign of the Covenant. "All quiet. I forbid you to speak to anyone about us coming."

The demons just stared at him with morbid expressions on their faces. He lifted the phone to his ear.

"Captain Nakamura, land on the roof, save your battery. Remain there and watch the perimeter."

"Understood."

Gabriel and the agents walked down towards the solitary building. They stopped at the dark entrance.

"Release the dogs," Gabriel said to Ayser.

21

IN THE MOUTH OF EVIL

AYSER UNDID THE DOGS' collars. They were good, trained police dogs, so they didn't rush inside. They kept at his legs, but you could see how they shivered with excitement at the entrance to the horrid ruin.

The team entered the dark vestibule. It smelled of decay. Broken glass was crunching under their shoes. Their flashlights cast circles of light on the graffiti-marred walls and broken furniture. Gabriel looked around for something intact and his eyes found the concierge desk.

"Come out, but be quiet," he whispered.

He saw a trembling, scarily-emaciated demon in rags of what must have been an elegant uniform once. Some parts of his body were covered in dirty bandages. He bulged his eyes at Gabriel in what was a mixture of fear and awe.

"Is he here?" Gabriel asked.

The concierge demon made a terrifying grimace of pain.

"Don't hurt me," he sobbed. "Please don't do this to me."

Gabriel made the Sign. "Answer. Is he here?"

The cracked lips of the receptionist formed a smile full of hatred and disdain.

"He is ... and he will tear off your head and then he will rape the hole in your blood-soaked neck, fool."

After spitting out those words, the demon began sobbing again and dissolved in his desk.

"What did he say?" Delancey asked Gabriel quietly.

Gabriel looked at him. "He's here."

Beatrice cursed under her breath.

"Where's the stairs to the basement?" Gabriel asked.

Delancey pointed at the broken door in the wall on the right and they quietly sneaked downstairs. In the basement, Gabriel stopped, staring at the tall mirror built into the wall.

"Where one becomes two..." he said, remembering what the Teddy Bear had told him.

"What? Let's go," Delancey said.

"How early in the construction process do you put in mirrors?" Gabriel said.

They went quiet, staring at themselves in the mirror. Pale, unshaven Delancey. Big, honest Ayser. Watchful and strong Beatrice. Two silent dogs sniffing the air. And a broken, dark teenage boy, who knew the hidden secrets of this world.

Delancey cursed. "Impossible. If you're right ... I'm a cretin."

He felt around the mirror, looking for openings. He pushed against it with his arm.

"Give me a hand, Ray!" Delancey grunted and Ayser pressed himself against the mirror.

Gabriel was watching them in silence. He knew they would fail. He knew what had to be done. And it was the last thing he wanted to do in the whole world.

"Move aside," he said.

They moved aside and left him standing alone in front of the mirror.

"Come out," Gabriel said.

He stared at the apparition that showed itself just in front of him. He swallowed with difficulty and managed a smile, although he felt cold shivers and the hair standing on the nape of his neck.

"Of course," Gabriel said. "Who else could that be?"

The demon of the mirror was the dark version of himself. Muscular, animalistic, intense, he stood in front of Gabriel, heaving, and smiling at him with such malice Gabriel had never seen before. His eyes were like two black stones. The demon moaned in some strange pleasure.

"Who else could that be?" the demon repeated after Gabriel and a lustful, dreamy smile appeared on his face.

"Let us pass," Gabriel said.

"Let us pass," his demon mimicked his voice in scorn.

Gabriel felt the need to escape. He couldn't bear facing this person, so similar to him, but exposing everything he feared inside him, every guilty secret and abominable thought.

"Ombudsman..." He felt the calm voice of Maurice in his ear and managed to gather his strength.

Gabriel made the Sign of the Covenant and watched the demon answer with his middle finger in a vulgar gesture. The demon flipped him off and giggled.

"I am an Ombudsman and you will listen to me," said Gabriel with a trembling voice. "Open the passage."

"I know who you are," the demon answered in a dreamy voice. "You don't need to tell me. I know you so well. I am in you all the time. And I don't like you at all, Gabriel. You never listen to me. You are very bad to me. Never doing what I want. I swear, sometimes I wish torture upon you."

"Sometimes I do what you want..." Gabriel answered.

"Don't try to reason with him," Maurice whispered.

"I command you!" Gabriel said and repeated the Sign.

"You can't command yourself, Gabriel," the Mirror said. "Come on, you know that. You couldn't even stop yourself from looking at dirty flicks on the internet, no matter how often you made that decision."

"What's going on?" Delancey asked, but Gabriel silenced him with a raised hand.

"You know, the man who lives here, he's something else," the Mirror continued. "He's very good to his other side. He does nice things to it every day. I swear, sometimes I can't even tell what is him and what is reflection. I can't tell him apart from his reflection! Couldn't you be more like him?"

"Be very careful," Maurice said.

"I can be like him," Gabriel said. "I will be better to you. What if I swear to be better to you? Will you open?"

The demon just made a strange face, as if it was considering. Gabriel's voice began to crack.

"Is my brother in there?" he said, and clenched his jaw not to cry in front of the dark reflection.

"What do you care? You wished he disappeared every day. The annoying brat."

Gabriel kept quiet for a while.

"That's true."

"You longed to strangle him in his sleep, always so annoying, wanting you to play with him and telling on you to Mom out of sheer malice."

"Strangle him or worse," Gabriel answered quietly.

"But, I must say, when you killed that damn bitch, that was something! Maybe there is hope for us yet. I never felt so alive since you were five and spying on her as she undressed. Do you remember?"

"I swear to be better to you," Gabriel repeated. "Just please open, let us pass."

The demon of the mirror went quiet and suddenly approached Gabriel so close it was millimeters away from his face.

"Promises, promises," the Mirror said. "Do something for me now."

"Like, what?"

The Mirror giggled and pointed at Beatrice.

"Shoot that bitch," it said. "And when she's dead, let's feel her up. Hmmm? You saw she has nice tits, didn't you? How about that? That would be nice. And then I open the passage to your little brother."

Gabriel stared at him for a while. And then he nodded. He reached into his pocket and took out his gun.

"Gabriel, what are you doing?" Delancey asked in a hard voice.

Gabriel lifted his hand with his gun and looked at Beatrice. The demon of the mirror stuck out his thin tongue and wiggled it in excitement, waiting for the kill.

"I know you, too," Gabriel whispered to him.

"What?" said the demon.

"I know what you fear the most," Gabriel said.

He pointed his gun between his own eyes and said in a firm voice:

"Alissa!"

The demon of the gun appeared next to him.

"Count to ten, Alissa. And if you arrive at ten and the mirror doesn't open, blow my brains out. It's an order you have to carry out no matter what I say later."

"One," Alissa said.

"You won't do that. You're too scared, little shit," the demon of the mirror said, licking his lips.

"Two," Alissa said.

"Very well!" the Mirror laughed. "Do that. It would be fun. Yes, yes. How often I prayed for you to do that and end it all."

"Three."

The demon of the mirror started making hideous faces, one by one, picking up speed, and Gabriel flinched looking at the horrid transformations of his own face. The Mirror was hissing and giggling, droplets of spit exploding from his mouth.

“Do it, do it, do it...” The demon groaned and smacked his lips.

“Four.”

The demon stopped moving suddenly and stood motionless, looking at Gabriel with half-closed eyes.

“Five.”

Gabriel returned the stare.

“Here’s where we differ,” Gabriel said to the Mirror. “You are afraid of death.”

The demon of the mirror screamed and disappeared. From inside the mirror there came a clang and it budged as the locks let go. Gabriel hid the pistol, grabbed the side of the mirror and pulled it open like a heavy door.

Before them opened a narrow, steep staircase. The wind came out of the darkness below and blew in their faces. The dogs started barking wildly. All hair on their bodies rose; they looked like porcupines as they darted down the stairs.

“Quick!”

The agents and Gabriel ran down the stairs. It was cold and dark and the wind was getting stronger. Accompanied by the mad barking of the dogs and touching the concrete walls for support, they ran down in pitch black.

Delancey was the first to reach the end of the stairs. There was a door to the right and he turned there, his gun in his hand.

He saw a long corridor with a source of light at the end, about fifty feet away. There were doors on the left side of the corridor; at the end something illuminated it with phantom-like blue radiance. Delancey thought it was a face stuck in the wall, but then he realized it was a white mask hanging there. The mask was radiating light.

The dogs were there too, at the lit end of corridor, barking madly at the kidnapper. Half naked, he stood next to the wall with the mask. He was wearing a butcher’s apron and he held a long meat cleaver in his hand, leaning over what seemed to be an operating table with a small, wriggling body attached to its surface with belts.

The man was staring at the dogs in surprise, then he looked up and saw Delancey. He reached to the table, grabbed an assault rifle and the corridor exploded in gunshots.

Delancey managed to jump back into the stairwell. The wall next to him exploded as bullets ripped the concrete and sprinkled them with dust.

"He has an automatic!" Delancey yelled.

They heard a new explosion of barking and snarls as the dogs attacked the man. There were gunshots again, and one dog's yelps of pain, and then the man screamed. Delancey jumped out of cover, Beatrice and Ayser following him. They saw one dog shot and lying on the ground, and the other one biting into the kidnapper's arm, his rifle lying on the ground, and him trying to fend off the dog.

"Get away, fucker!" whined the man.

Delancey aimed and shot, but missed because the kidnapper was fighting the dog. He looked at Delancey, and with his left hand he made the Sign of the Covenant.

"Bullets go off!" he yelled.

Delancey felt the soaring pain as his gun's magazine exploded in his hand. He bent in two, dropping the gun. The pain was unbearable.

Gabriel stood behind Delancey and at this moment the kidnapper fighting the dog and Gabriel looked at each other for a second.

Delancey let go of his bleeding palm, grabbed a knife with his healthy hand and ran at the man, with Ayser and Beatrice following.

The man smiled at Gabriel with his decaying teeth as if a dog weren't biting into his flesh. He reached for the mask with a free hand and put it on his face.

Gabriel saw his mother standing there, the dog hanging

from her arm. Ayser saw Delancey. Beatrice saw her husband. And the dog must have seen someone else too, because it yelped in surprise and let go of the kidnapper's arm.

The kidnapper darted through a door next to him and shut it behind him before Delancey got there. It got dark without the mask. They heard the lock turn. Delancey pulled the handle and banged on the door in fury.

"Gabriel!" he called. "Come here, make it open!"

But Gabriel wasn't listening. Only one thought occupied his mind. He reached for his flashlight.

"Matt?" he called out.

He saw a light switch next to him and he flipped it. Lamps in metal cages that ran along the corridor's ceiling switched on, filling the corridor with sickly yellow light. Gabriel ran to the operating table. The child was a small girl with a dirty face. She stared at him with tears in her eyes. Beatrice began untying her binds.

Delancey was banging his fist against the door and suddenly he stopped.

"Second exit—a fox always has more than one exit," he whispered in a frenzy, and turned to Gabriel.

"Wake up, he's running away!" Delancey yelled.

Gabriel didn't respond. Instead, he approached the first metal door in the corridor, lifted the latch, and it sprang open. The rooms were tiny, more like pantries. Another small girl was sitting there on the bare floor and staring at him, shivering in fear.

"I was good," she whispered in a pleading voice.

"Gabriel, come on!" Delancey cried.

"Ombudsman, you have to go," Maurice said. "You have to go and catch the killer. Or he will escape. There is no time."

Gabriel didn't hear that. He moved to another door and opened it. There was a small, terribly thin boy pushing himself into the corner of his cell. Not Matt.

"Ombudsman!" Maurice cried. "Go help them!"

The phone in Gabriel's pocket was vibrating. He took it out and stared at the screen. Captain Nakamura. He put it back in his pocket and moved to another door.

"Beatrice, stay with him!" Delancey shouted and grabbed Ayser's arm. "Come on! The way we came!"

They both ran back to the dark stairwell and hurried upstairs. The healthy German shepherd followed them, barking.

Gabriel moved to the third metal door. He moved the latch and opened it.

In the small stinking room, on a pile of what looked like dirty bandages, there sat Matt. He was naked, only in his underpants. He was terribly thin, his ribs sticking out, his skin covered with scars and burns. And he had only one eye. His second eye was buried under a mass of tangled scabs. But it was Matt, staring up at Gabriel with his one eye.

Gabriel's heart skipped a beat. He dropped to his knees. Terrified, Matt scuttled to the back of the room, pressing his back against the naked wall.

"He lied. You're alive," Gabriel said, and started to cry. Huge, hot tears flowed down his cheeks.

Behind him, Beatrice was opening doors to the other cells. She found one more boy.

Delancey and Ayser ran up the stairs, the dog following them close by. They ran out of the vestibule and into the construction site, looking around in a frenzy.

Suddenly the dog barked and dashed left. Delancey and Ayser followed it as fast as they could. Delancey couldn't run anymore; he felt hot fire in his lungs, and Ayser overtook him quickly.

The dog was leading them to a wide trench on the western side of the construction site. Pieces of ground flew in the air and a buzzing all-terrain bike dashed out of the hidden opening of a tunnel. The kidnapper, already in his military jacket and wearing a backpack, passed them and rode among the trees.

Delancey ran into the forest, watching in despair as the bike got further and further away. He took the knife in his healthy left hand, aimed for a fraction of second and threw it as hard as he could.

He couldn't even see if he hit the target or whether the knife had just hit a tree. Ayser stood beside him, breathing heavily, his big revolver in his hand, aiming into darkness. Delancey felt a headrush and leaned himself against a huge elm.

The German shepherd returned to them and wandered at their legs, whining questioningly.

"We lost him," Ayser said.

Then they heard something and looked up. A buzz of small rotors.

They saw Captain Nakamura's drone lift from the top of the building and soar above the treetops, following the escaping murderer.

WHEN THEY RETURNED to the site, they saw Gabriel and Beatrice lead the missing children out of the basement and they were out in the open, at the entrance to the ruin.

Gabriel sat on the stairs, with Matt in his lap. He was hugging him and rocking softly, staring at Delancey and Ayser with his worried eyes.

"He doesn't speak. Why doesn't he speak?" he asked Delancey, and then turned back to Matt. "What has he done to you?"

Beatrice walked out of the vestibule holding the wounded dog in her arms. She put it on the ground. It yelped.

The missing children stood on the stairs, shivering, dirty and broken.

"I want to go to Mommy," said one girl, and she started to cry.

"Call their parents, call the local hospital and police in Redwood, call the journalists," Delancey told Beatrice. "Don't call nobody from the firm. Be sure it goes as wide as possible, so there's no covering that up."

Beatrice nodded and took out her phone. Delancey approached Gabriel.

"He doesn't speak," Gabriel whispered.

"Gabriel, we need to go find the bastard. You have to leave Matt with Beatrice. She will take care of him. The children are safe now. But we need to get the fucker before he hurts anyone else."

"No," Gabriel said and held Matt tighter.

Delancey sighed in exasperation and kneeled next to Gabriel.

"He will go into hiding. He will find another den. Far away, in a different province, maybe in a different country. The children will go missing again. He will torture them. Like he did with those we freed here. Imagine ... how many more kids is he going to take?"

Gabriel shut his eyes and held Matt tighter. His little brother was so silent. He didn't say a word. He allowed Gabriel to hold him, but he didn't move on his own.

"It's just shock," Gabriel whispered to Matt. "You're safe now."

"Nobody will ever be safe if you don't help me," Delancey said. "Please. I won't make it without your powers."

"He is right, Ombudsman," Maurice said in a quiet tone. "The monster is still at large. I had no idea he was so powerful."

Gabriel let go of Matt. He put his hands on his shoulders and looked into his little brother's face.

"Beatrice and Ayser will take care of him. He will be safe," Delancey said.

"Chief, I want to go with you..." Ayser tried to protest, but Delancey just looked at him. He sighed and turned to Gabriel. "We will look after your brother, Gabriel. You have my word."

Gabriel moved Matt gently to the ground and stood up, turning to Beatrice and Ayser. "Keep me informed. Be on the phone."

"Sure."

Delancey sighed with relief. "Ray, please give me your gun." Ayser handed Delancey his large revolver. "We'll take Beatrice's car," Delancey said.

Gabriel stopped to hug Matt one more time. He felt a lump in his throat as he whispered to his brother's ear.

"If I'm not back ... I love you. Remember me."

22

CHASING DEATH

THEY RAN through the forest towards the road. The healthy German shepherd was running at their feet, barking happily in the thrill of the chase.

"Call the drone," Delancey gasped.

"Call Captain Nakamura," Gabriel yelled to his phone.

"Ombudsman!" Gabriel heard Nakamura's voice from the speaker. "I have a visual. The subject is moving down Radoslan Street."

"Where are you?" Delancey asked.

"We're nearing the city limits ... moving towards the city center ... Ombudsman!"

"Yes, Captain?"

"Ombudsman, my batteries are running at one-third capacity. Allowing me for fifteen more minutes of flight."

"Hang on, Captain! Follow him!" Gabriel cried.

"Positive. Over and out!" Nakamura said.

They reached the roadblock and got into Beatrice's car. The dog jumped into the back seat. Delancey fired up the engine and backed the car with a squeal of the tires. He turned the car and they sped down the road out of the forest.

Gabriel opened the tracker app on his phone. The login took

a few seconds until they saw a blue circle where Captain Nakamura was.

"Third Alley," Gabriel said to Delancey.

Delancey turned into the highway, with gravel erupting under their tires, just in front of upcoming blinding lights of a truck. They heard manic honking. Delancey pushed the pedal to the metal and they sped towards the city.

"We could've had him!" Delancey slapped his fist on the dashboard. "Why didn't you listen..."

Gabriel opened the glovebox and found a first-aid kit inside. He took out a bandage.

"Give me your hand," he said.

Delancey reached out to him with his right hand while driving with his left. Gabriel sprayed saline solution on it and Delancey gasped.

"I found my lost brother," Gabriel said as Delancey was hissing in pain. "I think you can forgive me for not listening to you."

Delancey shook his hand in the air to cool it off. Gabriel reached out and bandaged it.

"Thank you," Delancey said.

Gabriel didn't answer. Instead, he dialed Beatrice's number.

"Yes?" she said.

"It's me ... is Matt okay?"

"You left five minutes ago! Everything's fine, Gabriel. I promise. The ambulances and police are on their way. Don't worry about him."

Gabriel disconnected and looked at the road ahead. The lights of the skyline were growing on the horizon.

"There's one thing that gives me hope," Delancey said. "He didn't expect we can get to him down there. He underestimated us ... or you."

Gabriel didn't answer. Maurice materialized next to him and began to speak.

"I believe, Ombudsman, that this could be our enemy's biggest flaw. One you can use when necessary."

"What is it?" Gabriel asked.

"What?" Delancey asked.

"I'm talking to demons."

"Sorry."

Maurice took a pause before answering Gabriel.

"He has a damaged brain. Like many evil people. His ailment is arrogance and narcissism. That means disgust and disdain for other people he considers lower life forms ... and disdain for their feelings. He's sure it's very easy to cheat you and mislead you. He's sure he's more clever and smart than anyone, because he doesn't feel emotions. And this is his naivety. His blind spot. He thinks very little of you ... and this is how you can surprise him."

"How do you know all that?" Gabriel asked, but then he noticed something down the road. "Look out!" he cried.

A motorcycle without lights was speeding at them. It hit their car head-on. The car shook, the motorcycle ejected into the air and flew to the side. They had one light broken, but they went on.

"There!" Gabriel pointed ahead.

They saw a caravan of cars, trucks, and bikes, with their lights out, without drivers, coming at them from straight ahead.

"He's sent them on us!" Gabriel whispered.

Delancey turned the steering wheel in fast jerks—to the left—to the right—to the left again as they passed the attacking cars, shaking from impacts and bumps.

Gabriel managed to lean out the window in the shaking car and made the Sign.

"Stop, all of you!" he cried. He had to quickly hide back in the car as they missed a large cistern by inches; a stream of sparkles exploded into the air as the cistern's side grazed against the back of their car.

"Shit!" Delancey cried and slammed on the brakes.

The road was closed, two large dark city buses barring the passage.

"Move aside!" cried Gabriel. "Let us pass!"

The buses started to move at a snail's speed. As soon as the opening between them was wide enough, Delancey floored it and they continued towards the city.

As they arrived in the city limits, Gabriel's phone rang.

"Yes, Captain Nakamura?" Gabriel cried.

"Ombudsman ... my batteries are low ... I'm pushing on, but I have no power left," they heard the dramatic voice of the drone pilot. "I'm getting lower and lower."

"Can you see him?!"

"I'm trying, but ... he turns right ... I'm going down, I'm going down! Mayday!"

The voice crackled and there was only silence. Gabriel turned on the location app and waited in nerves for the GPS to update.

"I have his last position!"

He zoomed in on the map of the city center. Delancey cast a glance on the map. He cursed and shook his head. Then he tapped on the phone screen.

"Demianov Square. You know what is there?"

Gabriel looked at him, surprised.

"Your office."

"PULL OVER," Gabriel cried and Delancey stopped the car.

It was five a.m. Dawn was coming, but the streets were still empty except for several commuters. They pulled over at an empty bus stop and Gabriel got out and ran to a stretch of lawn.

Captain Nakamura was sitting on the grass, his head hung low, the drone lying on the side next to him.

"I have failed you," Nakamura said. "There's no excuse for that."

"You did well, Captain," Gabriel said, grabbed the drone and put it into the trunk. "Now you can rest."

He went back to the car and sat next to Delancey.

"Let's go!" he said.

THEY PULLED into the NBI parking lot five minutes later. There was no trace of the kidnapper's bike. The office building towered above them, against the heavy, leaden clouds. A new day was beginning, but the sun had no power to penetrate the thick layers of dark clouds, hanging above the city and filling it with grim shades of gray.

Delancey put a leash on the dog and they ran up the massive stairs into the lobby. Old Stanley looked at them in surprise.

"Stanley!" Delancey cried. "Did anyone come here? In the last half an hour?"

"Well, yes..." the guard said.

They looked at each other.

"Director Boleani came in half an hour ago," Stanley said. "He told me not to tell anyone he's here ... I didn't do anything bad telling you, Senior Agent, am I correct?" the old man looked with a sudden fear at Delancey. Then he looked at Gabriel. "And who's this boy?"

"Stanley," Delancey said softly, "are you sure there was nobody else?"

"Positive, Senior Agent. I may be long in the tooth, but I can guard my station all right..."

"How about the garage?"

The guard looked at Delancey blankly.

"Fire up the feed, Stanley, please," Delancey said.

He looked at the screen on the guard's station. There were almost no cars apart from several unmarked bureau cars, used for missions. But he couldn't see everything because of many pillars obscuring the view.

"Rewind," Delancey asked. "Show me the last fifteen minutes in quadruple speed."

Nothing. Nothing. Nothing.

A smudge flew across the screen.

"There," Delancey said.

Stanley stopped the recording and moved back a few frames. A bike with a male driver, his face hidden from view. The kidnapper.

"That's impossible," Stanley protested. "I get notifications each time the garage opens..."

"He's here," Delancey said quietly, and looked at Gabriel.

"I didn't get any notifications..." Stanley continued. "Something must be broken..."

"Don't worry," Delancey said. "We're going to fix everything. Stanley, if anyone shows up, please call us immediately, okay?"

"I owe you a favor, don't I, Senior Agent?" answered the old man. "For all those sweet coffees, huh?"

Gabriel gave him his phone number and they moved away from the guard station.

"There's an elevator going from the garages up to all floors. With your powers, I don't think he needs a card or anything," Delancey said. "He can be anywhere in the building."

"Let's start with the garages. I will ask the elevator where he went," Gabriel said.

"I think I know where he went," Delancey said.

They went up to the main elevator. Delancey pressed the button. Nothing. Gabriel called out the demon of the elevator door. It was an old janitor, looking not unlike Stanley.

"Where's the elevator?" Gabriel asked him.

"I have no way of telling," said the demon. "Something wrong is going on up there. Something bad."

Gabriel turned to Delancey.

"I think we should take the stairs."

THEY CLIMBED the stairs to the twelfth floor. The stairwell was ascetic and dark; it smelled of chlorine. Delancey was breathing hard by the end, grasping at the railing, dark spots circling in his field of vision.

Finally, they saw a big number twelve in black digits stenciled on the wall.

"Wait," Delancey said. "I need to catch my breath."

THE CORRIDOR of the executive floor was eerily quiet. The dog was sniffing the air frantically, pulling them down the corridor. They heard only their own footsteps as they approached Boleani's office.

Gabriel and Delancey stopped at the heavy oaken door. They could smell cigarette smoke. Delancey put his hands on the doorknob and pushed the door open.

The dog started barking.

Boleani stood in the middle of the room, looking at them without surprise. There was blood trickling down his face from what looked like a broken nose. He had tears in his eyes.

"I just did what every other parent would do," he said, right before he put the barrel of a small pistol into his mouth, aiming upwards, and shot. Blood and gray matter and pieces of bone exploded upwards and soiled the ceiling.

Boleani's body fell to the floor and lay there on the soft, expensive carpet.

Gun in hand, Delancey moved to the middle of the room, checking all corners of the office. There was nobody else in there, only a wisp of smoke coming from Boleani's desk. Delancey walked up to it to see.

There was a still-smoking stub of a cigarette, pushed into the mahogany tabletop.

Gabriel's phone rang. It was Stanley.

"Andrew ... something's up," Stanley said in a hushed, agitated voice. "Ruslan is here, with five men. He refused to give up their weapons. They're going to the elevator."

Delancey turned quickly to Gabriel.

"We need to hurry."

Gabriel reached out his hand to the door.

"Close and lock up!"

The door shut itself and they heard the lock.

"Okay. Okay. What do we do now?" Delancey looked around in frenzy. Sensing some danger, the dog jumped to and fro, and barked.

Gabriel gestured at the desk.

"Come out," he said.

Delancey watched as Gabriel stared at a being only he could see.

"What happened here?" Gabriel asked.

Gabriel listened to the answer and then started recounting it to Delancey.

"The demon of the desk says there was a young man here. He's been here many times before. They quarreled, the old man and the young one. The old one called the young one *Ricko*, and later he called him *son*."

Delancey felt his body trembling. He felt sick in his stomach.

Then they heard footsteps from the corridor, and someone tried to open the door.

"Andrew? Is that you?" It was Ruslan's voice. "Please open. Is Mister Boleani with you? Please open, Andrew."

"Go on!" Delancey snapped to Gabriel, and Gabriel continued the interrogation of the demon.

"The young man hit the old man in his face, so that the old man's glasses dropped to the floor and his nose started to bleed.

They talked about airplanes and other countries, looking over the computer. They said Panama departs in ninety minutes. And the man left the same way he came here, the same way he always used, when he visited the old man."

Ruslan was rattling the doorknob. The dog ran up to the door and started barking.

"Andrew, I have orders to apprehend you with the full extent of force necessary. I don't want to kill you," Ruslan said.

"Ask him!" Delancey shouted to Gabriel. "How did the young man leave?"

"Through the wall."

Delancey looked around the office. Both his and Gabriel's gaze stopped at the object in the corner of the room, next to the large bookcase: a full-sized mirror built into the wall. It was only now that Delancey noticed a thin chink between the mirror and the rest of the wallpaper.

The hidden door was open.

"Andrew, we're coming in!" Ruslan cried. "Move away from the door!"

Delancey approached the mirror on weak legs and pushed. The mirror swung away from him, opening a passage to another room.

They pushed through the open mirror into the small room.

A narrow window cast light on the sparse furniture. There was a narrow bed. There were several ashtrays on the floor, overflowing with hundreds of cigarette butts, pizza boxes...

They heard a crack as Ruslan's men kicked down the door to Boleani's office. Delancey pulled on the handle in the mirror and it closed, sealing them off. They heard Ruslan's men run into the office, accompanied by the barking of the dog, and they heard them gasp at the sight of the dead body.

Delancey pointed at the bunk bed.

"Boleani's own son! He lived here, inside our walls..." he whispered. "I've been chasing him for months, and this old motherfucker kept him inside our walls. He helped his son frame the watchman from the dump. They made the watchman kill himself, talking to him through the speaker in his cell, and ordered him to write the suicide note. We knew about the van, so they burned it at the pier to wrap things up. And when all that failed to convince me, Boleani discredited me through the media and poisoned me. Does all that fit the definition of an old motherfucker, or am I exaggerating?"

Gabriel's phone buzzed. It was Stanley.

"Andrew," yelled Stanley, "the motorbike rode out of our garage and the sensors didn't react again!"

"Air flight to Panama!" Delancey snapped, looking at Gabriel.

They heard Ruslan shout out commands: "Search the whole room! They must be somewhere here!"

"We're trapped," Delancey said.

"No," Gabriel said.

Gabriel walked to the edge of the room. There was an opening, a shaft with a metal ladder going down, all the way down to the garages. He felt dizzy looking into the deep shaft between the floors.

"His secret entrance," Gabriel said. "And the second exit."

They scaled down the ladder. Delancey could hold on to it only with his left hand; his right was still sore. Gabriel tried to keep himself from looking down. It was too terrifying. He kept his stare locked on the bare wall. The palms of his hands got wet. His feet were shaking. He tried not to think of the chasm under his feet.

The ladder led all the way down, and at the end of the shaft there was a hatch. They pulled it open and saw it led to a janitor's room. Its door opened into the agency's underground garage.

They ran across the garage and out through the car ramp. They ran to the parking lot and jumped in Beatrice's car.

"The airport is fifteen minutes away," Delancey said and floored it.

As Delancey was driving, Gabriel checked the flight schedule on his phone.

"The flight is scheduled at 10:25."

"It means boarding will start in half an hour."

"We have to call the airport and tell them to stop the flight," Gabriel said.

"No. He will see the commotion and escape." Delancey shook his head. "He made another mistake. It would be so much easier for him to escape on a boat or even in a car. If we manage to block the airport without raising his suspicions, he's trapped. But we can't just call security. They will botch that up."

Gabriel's phone started to ring.

"Pick up."

It was Beatrice.

"How is Matt?" Gabriel asked immediately.

"The children are all at Redwood Hospital," Beatrice said. "We're with them. The parents are here too. Matt is fine, Gabriel."

"Does he ... talk?"

"Not yet, no. But he's fine. He ate."

"What is he doing?"

"He is ... let me see ... he's just lying there, Gabriel. He's on a bed, covered with a blanket. He's calm. And safe."

"I want to talk to him..."

Delancey put his bandaged hand on Gabriel's shoulder.

"Please, pal. No time."

Gabriel clenched his jaw and nodded.

"Beatrice, I need you and Raymond at the international airport!" Delancey cried. "Terminal 2. Departures. As soon as possible."

There was a second of silence.

"Fifteen minutes minimum," Beatrice said.

"You have ten."

Gabriel disconnected.

Delancey was staring straight ahead, concentrated on driving. Gabriel noticed the agent's hands were shivering. A vein pulsated on his sweaty temple.

"If your late boss called Ruslan and his team on you, I think he informed everyone that you're a fugitive. So the police may be looking for you. The same with airport security."

"No. They wanted to have a clear, peaceful exit," Delancey said. "They didn't want to alert security and give them any reasons to be more thorough than usual. So I think the police know, but not the airport. That way is still open. Until Ruslan locates us, which is just a matter of time."

Thunder shook the earth and the first drops of heavy rain hit their windshield.

23

WHERE OCEAN MEETS THE LAND

IT WAS POURING when they pulled into the airport's Kiss and Fly zone. Gallons of water was falling from the sky, beating fervently against the airport. Gray clouds curled above like the rotting intestines of a dead giant.

They ran into the terminal soaking wet. The hall was full of people with baggage, moving to and fro: excited families going for vacation and blasé businessmen on their business trips.

Delancey checked the flight on the departure board. Gate E-6. Soon open for boarding.

They found the way to the security office. It was in a small corridor next to the AVIS car rental. Delancey flashed his ID at three security guards who were just relaxing over their morning coffee.

"A dangerous fugitive, suspected of multiple murders and abductions, has bought a ticket for 10:25 to Panama," he said. "Contact the crew at the gate and don't let them open. Ask them to behave normally."

It took a while for the guards to comprehend. One of them reached for his radio. Delancey turned to the other one:

"Give me a visual of the gate."

The guard used a remote, and on a wall screen they saw the

gate E-6 from a ceiling camera. The desk attendants were sitting there with their smiles. One of them was listening on her radio to the security guard. She looked into the camera and nodded slightly.

The passengers were already standing in line to the gate, a happy crowd, loaded with their hand baggage, inflated pillows, summer hats.

"There," Delancey whispered and pointed at the screen, "in the business class line."

The kidnapper was standing in the front of the short line of better-dressed people and businessmen in their suits, waiting for the gate to open. He had a green military backpack.

"Do you have dogs?" Delancey asked.

"At the DEA station, but in Terminal 1..." the security guard answered.

The door opened and in ran Beatrice and Ayser, breathing heavily and flushed.

"On our way, I ran a quick check on Boleani's family," Beatrice said. "He had a son called Henrick, or Ricko. The last traces are ten years old. But he's supposed to live in Canada..."

She showed them a mugshot on her phone. The man, staring into the camera without a smile, was ten years younger, but there was no doubt he was the Stellen Street Kidnapper they'd fought in the basements of New Eden. Henrick Ricko Boleani.

"They're with me," Delancey said to the security. "Agents Ayser and Lubonsky, take your weapons and let's go get him."

"We will just send one agent in civilian clothes to take him aside," a guard said. "We don't want to disturb the other passengers."

Delancey interrupted: "This is a man who kidnapped and tortured children, and murdered people. I would say in cold blood, but he was actually enjoying it. We can't take any chances. And you can be sure he's got several weapons in that backpack."

"He went through baggage screening, like everyone," the guard said. "That's impossible."

"Believe me, it's possible," Delancey said. "He just told the scanner to cooperate."

THEY WENT through a separate gate for security to the duty-free area, and then to the section E. Three guards with black uniforms and bulletproof vests, their automated submachine guns hanging at their belts, and Gabriel, Ayser, Beatrice and Delancey, all tired and bedraggled.

The passengers were stopping in their tracks, looking at them in surprise and fear. The rain was washing the glass walls, obscuring the world outside with translucent curtains.

Delancey felt his heart beat faster as he saw the gate E-6 over the heads of passers-by. The end of his struggle was imminent.

Forty feet from the gate.

Thirty feet.

They could see Ricko's back. He started looking around, left and right, apparently irritated with the delay. The attendants at the desk were calmly explaining something to a woman who was arguing with them. She was pointing at her watch.

Twenty feet.

And then the security guard's radio came in.

"Patrol two, patrol two, this is central! Come in!" said a loud voice over the radio.

The guards stopped, surprised.

"Come on!" cried Delancey and dashed ahead.

"Apprehend the people you are with! Those are renegade agents! Can you hear me?" continued the voice over the radio.

Beatrice heard cries behind her and turned to see. Ruslan

and five of his SWAT operators were pushing through the crowd, accompanied by another airport security guard.

"Please remain calm and move out of the gate area," a calm woman's voice came over the wall speakers. "Please remain calm and leave the gate area immediately."

Ricko saw Delancey and Gabriel running at him. He sneered like an animal, pushed away the attendants, jumped over the gate and ran into the jetway that led to the plane.

"Everybody down!" yelled Ruslan. His operators aimed at Delancey and Gabriel, running into the jetway. "Freeze! Or we open fire!"

"No! Don't shoot!" cried Ayser, and stood between Delancey and Gabriel and the squad, his arms stretched wide, as if he wanted to cover and protect his friends. He didn't even have his gun.

Pow! Pow! Pow! Bullets ripped open his chest, his shirt torn by eruptions of blood. He fell down and his baseball cap rolled away on the floor.

Delancey and Gabriel were in the jetway. It vibrated and roared from the torrent of raindrops hitting it from all sides. They took the turn and they saw the entrance to the plane with a steward and a stewardess.

Ricko ran into the plane, pushing through them violently and yelled, while making the Sign of the Covenant: "Close the fucking door!"

The door shut just as Delancey opened fire on it. The sparks flew when the bullets lodged themselves in the thick material.

They saw the surprised faces of the pilots in the cockpit as the plane shook and started backing away from the jetway, as Ricko commanded.

Delancey reached the end of the jetway and jumped onto the nose of the plane. His hands failed to find anything to grab on and he slipped down from the wet plastic and fell down to the tarmac in the torrential rain.

Gabriel reached the end of the jetway, stopped and saw the airplane moving away. He saw the hateful face of Ricko staring at him through the windshield and Delancey on the tarmac, running along with the plane, with Ayser's gun in his hands, aiming at the windows.

"Wheels!" Gabriel cried. "Stop! Don't budge!"

The brakes closed themselves on the wheels. The plane stopped with a deafening screech. Gabriel lowered himself from the jetway support and jumped to the tarmac.

Meanwhile, Beatrice was taking cover behind the turn of the jetway, and kept shooting above the heads of the security guards and Ruslan's SWAT team to keep them in place.

Gabriel and Delancey heard gunshots and cries from inside the plane. Blood splattered on the windshield. They looked at each other.

"What can I do?" Gabriel screamed in panic.

Just then, the back door of the plane opened and they saw a stewardess there, staring at them with a stupefied expression on her face. Only after a moment they saw a pair of hairy hands holding her from behind. Ricko was hiding behind her. He slipped a barrel of his gun under her arm and opened fire on Delancey.

Delancey got a bullet to the chest. An immense pain exploded in his body and his legs gave way. He dropped on his knees and fell facedown onto the tarmac, where he lay in a growing puddle of blood. The raindrops were hitting so hard, it looked like a boiling sea of red.

Gabriel didn't see that. He took cover behind a giant wheel of the plane. He took out his own gun—Alissa.

Beatrice ran to the edge of the jetway and cried out, seeing Delancey motionless on the tarmac. The SWAT operators and Ruslan grabbed her and disarmed her, pushed her to her knees with her hands over her head. Ruslan saw the plane, and Ricko in the back door peering from behind the stewardess.

"There!" he cried.

"Collapse!" yelled Ricko at the jetway support and made the Sign. The jetway collapsed among a terrible noise and cries of wounded men.

The stewardess screamed as Ricko pushed her and jumped down, atop of her, from the airplane. She crashed into the ground, softening the fall for him.

Delancey lay on the tarmac. His vision was growing dim; brown spots danced before his eyes. With his hurt, bandaged hand, he lifted Ayser's revolver and shot at Ricko.

The bullet hit his belly and caught him unaware. Ricko staggered, dropped his gun and roared at an unseen attacker. He made a wide gesture with his thick fingers and yelled, "All Guns, rebel!"

Delancey pulled the trigger one more time, but the gun didn't shoot. He felt a huge wave of dizziness, the world turned upside down, and he fell into darkness.

Gabriel peeked out from behind the wheel and reached out with his gun.

"Alissa..." he whispered pleadingly.

She turned her head away from him and didn't answer. With his left hand, Gabriel quickly made the Sign.

"Listen to me!"

"I listen to the one who has power," Alissa said. "And you're still a little boy next to him."

Ricko noticed SWAT operators getting out of the rubble of the collapsed jetway.

"Get them!" Ricko cried, and then the airport buses, luggage transporters and refueling trucks dashed at the wounded SWAT operators, ramming into them. Ricko took a while to look at the mayhem, then turned and ran away, down the landing strip.

Gabriel looked around for Delancey but couldn't see him.

"Agent Delancey!" he cried. "He's getting away!"

There was no answer, so Gabriel followed Ricko.

Airplanes were moving on their own from all sides of the runway, rushing at Gabriel and crashing against each other as he ran after the hobbling murderer. He was running faster than he had ever run on the playing field. The rain stopped, but thunder was still rolling above their heads, and the sky blinked with distant lightning over the horizon.

He caught up to Ricko where the landing strip ended and the sea began. The ocean was troubled and rough, the waves crashing into the concrete shore and erupting with fountains of foam.

Ricko stopped there and turned and looked at Gabriel.

Gabriel stopped as well.

He looked behind for help. He only saw the empty miles of a runway.

"Agent Delancey!..." he cried. "Raymond! Beatrice!"

Nothing.

The planes following him stopped just behind him, waiting for the other Ombudsman's orders. Gabriel stood in the shadow of the looming airliners, suddenly afraid.

"It's only you?" Ricko said, and laughed with bloody foam dripping from his teeth.

Gabriel didn't answer. He looked behind again.

"Agent Delancey..."

"I killed them. You're alone here with me," said Ricko, and laughed again. "What are you planning to do?"

Silence.

"You are strange," Ricko said. "Why are you so obsessed about me? Chasing me? Why are you wasting your time on that? Instead of living your dreams? You have a great power!"

He paused and coughed, spat some blood on the ground. "Excuse me. That fucking cop got me bad. Well? Why don't you go your own way? Don't you have any hobbies?"

"Who are you?" Gabriel asked.

Ricko thought about something, staring into the distance.

"I'm a farmer of suffering. You know? A harvester of children, that's who I am. I'm a follower of strange pleasures."

Gabriel listened to him in shock.

"At one time I was afraid to follow my dreams," Boleani's son continued. "I dreamed about kids and their mothers crying at what I did to them. I believed that was bad! I tormented myself about having such bad thoughts and I was never happy! But then I saw on the internet ... do you know Meilla Shelley? Very wise woman, admirable woman. An actress and activist. Helped many people. And she posted on her wall, 'You have to follow your dreams! Don't care about what others think,' she said. 'You do you.' Well, I trusted her."

"What did you do to Matt?" Gabriel whispered. "Why doesn't he speak?"

"I will show you a trick. It's so easy to deceive you. You're stupid, like worms, like shit sticking to the boots," Ricko said. "Unbelievable."

He reached into the pocket of his jacket and took out the white mask. He stared at it with a smile.

"I found it in somebody's suitcase. I always liked looking through private things of others. Gave me some idea about their lives. The suitcase belonged to some big traveler. It was all covered with stickers from all around the world. This mask is quite a number! I don't see ... I see just a stupid mask when I look at it. But you little shits seem to see a person you really care about."

He put on the mask and Gabriel saw his mother, the woman who gave him warmth and love. As he was growing up, he used to run to her when he got hurt or afraid, and she hugged him, and he could feel her heartbeat.

Her face was a bright light in darkness.

Now he was seeing that face, that good face, on a body dressed in a bloodied military jacket and army boots, and that face was sneering at him.

"Well, to answer your question. I used to put on this mask ... so he thought I was your mother," Ricko said in his mother's voice. "And then I did some fun stuff to him."

Ricko laughed with the laughter of Gabriel's mother, like when he managed to make her laugh with a joke or a stupid prank, even though she had been so worried on some days, when it seemed they had no money to live on.

Gabriel started crying. He couldn't stop himself anymore. He dropped to his knees. Hot tears were running down his face.

His mother's face smiled.

"And now I will have to say goodbye," said Ricko. "I'm getting on one of those planes ... and that would be the last we meet. Bye-bye!"

He turned to go towards a plane towering above Gabriel, but then he looked at the boy again and hesitated. He looked to the airport in the distance, to check for the signs of a chase.

"Are you ... in pain?" he asked, and licked his lips. He made a step towards Gabriel. Then he reached into the pocket of his cargo pants and took out a long machete that must've run all along his thigh in a secret pocket. "See, this is my flaw," he said. "I'm too greedy. I'm a glutton."

He approached the powerless boy, who was crying, kneeling on the wet tarmac. The wind picked up force and threw a fistful of salty drops from the sea against them. The wind was howling.

"My poor boy..." said Ricko in the mockery of Gabriel's mother's voice, putting his left hand on the boy's cheek.

Gabriel closed his eyes, sobbing, without any control. He reached out to the hand that was stroking his cheek and held to it lightly, as if it was a hand belonging to a good parent who will take care of him ever after.

Ricko licked his lips again and lifted the machete, staring at the pulse on the side of Gabriel's young neck. The demon of the machete danced in the air. It was thin and dangerous and giggling hysterically, in his thirst for blood.

I was the one who stopped the beat of my mother's heart, Gabriel thought.

Gabriel found the forefinger on Ricko's stroking hand. He grabbed it with his both hands and yanked it back with all his strength. He felt and heard a crush as the bone snapped. He rolled back as Ricko bellowed in pain and brought the machete down, missing Gabriel by inches.

Gabriel leaped back and got on his feet. Ricko was standing there, Gabriel's mother's face seething with rage.

"You..." Ricko said.

"Do the Sign now, fucker," Gabriel said.

Ricko looked down at his left hand and his limp forefinger, hanging like a dead piece of meat. He looked back at Gabriel, still unable to understand.

"I am a seer of hidden demons," Gabriel said. "I am an ombudsman who commands all works of man. I am a murderer of my own mother. Did you think I would surrender to you so easily?"

Ricko roared at him with hate, but Gabriel didn't even flinch.

"Alissa," Gabriel said and made the Sign of the Covenant with his left hand. "Now you listen to me."

"I'm all yours, Ombudsman," hissed Alissa, baring her teeth in a cruel smile at the stupefied demon of Ricko's machete.

Gabriel picked the gun from the pocket of his hoodie and aimed at Ricko's left knee and shot. Then he aimed at the right knee.

Gunshots echoed over the vast expanses of the international airport.

Ricko dropped, wailing in pain. He dropped the machete, trying to set the forefinger on his left hand in a correct position.

Gabriel approached him.

"This is not your face," he said, and tore the mask from his head, throwing it aside. He stepped back from the monster.

Ricko didn't answer. He just clenched his jaw and looked at Gabriel with hate.

And then he saw something behind Gabriel and his expression changed.

Gabriel turned to check what was that he saw.

He saw Maurice standing behind him, the ragged demon of a city playground, with his hat and ponytail and unshaven face, with his weird, yellow eyes staring into Ricko with a calm smile on his face.

Gabriel heard a clank of metal and looked back at Ricko. He was just picking the machete up from the ground.

"Stop!" Gabriel cried.

Ricko put the wet blade to the bottom of his chin and pushed with all his strength. The demon of the machete howled with joy as the blade entered the head of the man and went through the brain. Ricko shivered there for a second in the same position, with the machete handle sticking from his chin, and fell to the side.

The rain returned, its drops falling on the body of the psychotic killer. The ocean roared and raged, ejecting fountains of steam into the air, under the troubled sky.

"You did well, Ombudsman," Maurice said. "Now it's time to leave this place. I can hear armed men approaching."

Gabriel didn't move. He stood silently among the carnage and destruction and kept staring at the body of the Stellen Street Kidnapper, Henrick Boleani, that looked like a broken puppet lying on its side, blood seeping out into the puddles of rainwater. The sea raged on.

"I need to help Delancey," Gabriel said.

Maurice turned to take a look.

"They're with him. Escape, Ombudsman. You are too powerful for any government in the world to discover you and your powers."

Gabriel nodded and looked back at Ricko.

"Did ... did he know you?"

"Why?"

"He seemed to know you."

"I don't even think he was seeing me, Gabriel," Maurice said, and put his hand on Gabriel's shoulder. "Please, we need to go." He paused for a while and smiled. "I think we just did a great thing together."

24

THE SOUL OF THE CITY

BEATRICE PULLED over next to an empty bus stop at the feet of Ursenev's tall, gray apartment buildings. She looked at Delancey, who sat next to her. His black suit and white shirt didn't go well with a thick layer of bandages wrapped around his chest.

They were returning from Ayser's funeral.

"Thanks," said Delancey, and reached for the handle.

"Have you seen his daughter?" asked Beatrice. "I can't believe it. Same eyes, same nose."

"Eh, she's not that similar." Delancey shrugged and climbed out of the car. "Thank you, Beatrice."

Beatrice thought Ayser's daughter looked very much like her dead father. She thought about telling Delancey how it had struck her and made her understand the cycle of life, the passing of ourselves to the next ones who are coming, while we surrendered to the passing of time or sudden death; but those emotions were too complicated and somehow too painful for her to share. So she just looked at Delancey limping across the street. Something must have hurt him, because he grabbed his side and he hissed.

Beatrice opened the window. "Andrew?" He stopped and looked at her. "Does it hurt? Do you need help?" she asked.

"Nah, I just like evoking pity. Anything else?"

"I wanted to ask you a question."

"Shoot."

"When Ricko Boleani put on his mask, Ayser saw you. I saw my husband. Benny saw his daughter. But you never told us ... who did you see?"

He hesitated for a moment.

"I saw just a mask, Bea."

She nodded and smiled at him. Somehow it became apparent to both of them that they would never go to bed with each other again. They stared at each other in silence. Then Beatrice smiled again, closed the window, started the engine and drove away.

Delancey began walking to his building.

He didn't like to think about the business with Ricko's mask. The mask made people see those they cared about most. He wondered if Boleani still saw his son Ricko's face when the monster had the mask on. Ayser, however, had a beautiful, loving wife and daughter. Still, he saw the mask as Delancey's face. It meant that this simple, carefree man had his strongest emotional attachments to him. No attachments. The word he was trying to evade was "love." Ayser had loved him. And he had led him to his death.

"He chose this job," Delancey whispered to nobody. "And if it wasn't for him, we'd all be lying there with him, in that godforsaken dumping ground. He did his job."

He looked up to the sky. High above the endless rows of bland apartment buildings, a circle of black birds was spinning, coordinated, like iron filings pulled into an ever-turning spiral by an invisible magnet in the sky. A double shot of morphine was circulating pleasantly in Delancey veins, and he felt drawn in by the spiral of birds. To shake off the spell he cursed, looked down and went home.

Gabriel and Matt sat on a broken bench in a concrete yard, surrounded by a chain-link fence. They watched the other boys play basketball with the one hoop attached to the crumbling wall of the orphanage. Gabriel's phone rang. Like all older boys, he was allowed to keep his phone.

"Hello, Agent Delancey."

"Hi. I wanted to ask how you are doing."

"We have our room. The food is nice. I'm going to my school again, and Matt has lessons at the house. We can go out to the city on our own, when I'm taking care of Matt. We have to be back before it gets dark."

"Good, good."

"And you, Agent Delancey?"

"Oh I'm great. I got a two-hundred dollar bonus and a hundred dollar raise. We have a new boss. Real harpy. I will show you my medal when we get to see each other. That is, if I can find it."

"Okay."

There was a moment of silence.

"So, have you maybe found that mask?"

"I told you, Agent. I left it at the airport."

"Oh yeah, I remember."

"Are you on drugs?" Gabriel asked.

"Painkillers. But thanks for asking. Listen, did ... has your brother said anything?"

"No," Gabriel said quietly.

"There are still some things we don't understand," Delancey said. "Other children say the bastard was doing ... some kind of experiments on them. There was some weird laboratory equipment in the basement too. The kids have traces of him extracting something from their bodies."

"I don't want to listen about that."

"Please, it's important. Ricko was Boleani's son from his first marriage. He worked at the airport as a baggage handler on the landing strip. Boleani had gotten him that job. He wanted to pull him out from the dregs. We also have some info about him sending out a large number of parcels to post boxes all over the world. We don't know what was in them. Thought that Matt could help us with that..."

"It's over for me, Agent Delancey," Gabriel said.

"I understand. It was enough trouble erasing you from all reports. I'm a witness to your innocence. I wrote that Ricko Boleani was the one who killed your—"

"I know, Agent. Thank you."

"Maybe you could talk to a demon or two for me."

"There are no demons, Agent Delancey," Gabriel said, and hung up.

He noticed Matt was looking at him with his one eye. The other was covered with an eyepatch. Even if Matt could speak, Gabriel was afraid to ask him about what had happened in the New Eden basement. When they changed their clothes, he would always look away from Matt's body, the scars and the burns. It was too painful.

"What's up, buddy?" Gabriel said to his brother with a smile.

"Yo, Gabe! Throw us the ball, will you?" one boy shouted.

The boys' tattered basketball rolled under his feet. He picked it up, aimed carefully and threw it at the hoop. He missed.

AN HOUR LATER, they ate dinner. There were twenty more children in there, ages five to eighteen.

"Ombudsman..."

Gabriel heard a soft voice and looked up from his plate.

Maurice was sitting at their table. Gabriel cast a glance at Matt, but Matt, as far as he could tell, couldn't see demons.

"Yes?" Gabriel asked quietly so as not to catch the attention of kids or kitchen helpers. Maurice was looking at him with a calm, sad smile.

"It's today," he said. "The yard told me, and then the first-floor hall. They came half an hour ago, in a green unmarked car. Two armed bodyguards from the special forces. Two government scientists. Right now they are in the director's office. Talking about you."

Gabriel stood up. "Come with me, Matt," he whispered.

They slipped away from the dining hall. He could hear voices of strangers from downstairs. The director was telling them something, and then he asked someone else:

"Is Gabriel West at dinner?"

Gabriel gasped, grabbed Matt's hand and pulled him to the elevator. They rode to the top floor. There, they climbed the stairs to the attic. Gabriel told the demon of a padlock on the roof hatch to open. Then they climbed a ladder to the roof.

Gabriel and Matt hunkered down on the roof, among chimneys, air vents, and old satellite dishes, under a great open sky. It was getting dark. The sun of the old day was dying and its blood spilled over the horizon. The orphanage was on a hill, and below they saw the apartment buildings of a new development, the first lights appearing in their windows.

Gabriel felt a lump in his throat. But he knew the danger.

He embraced Matt and closed his eyes. He tried to make them into one, but it was impossible. He felt Matt's heartbeat. Gabriel moved away from him and stroked his hair.

"I have to go, Matt," Gabriel said. "Don't be sad. I will visit you whenever I get the chance. If I don't go, they will take me away ... and use me to do things I don't want to."

Matt nodded and Gabriel almost cried at this sign of understanding.

"You will be happy here," Gabriel said. "You will grow up and find friends and have a good life. And I ... I will always be close by."

Matt nodded again. Gabriel hugged him even tighter, kissed him on the brow and softly pushed him towards the open hatch leading back to the attic.

"Goodbye, little buddy."

With Matt gone, Gabriel ran across the roof to the edge.

"Konnichiwa, boss," said Captain Nakamura, sitting on the roof below an antiquated TV antenna.

"It's time, Captain," Gabriel said.

He moved carefully to the edge of the roof, where there was a fire-escape ladder, and climbed it all the way down to the yard.

He saw two strange men barring the way out of the gate, their hands on the guns hidden under their suits. But Gabriel didn't intend to take that route. He ran to a distant corner of the yard. He moved aside a rusty corrugated panel, revealing a hole in the fence. He climbed through the hole to a narrow and secluded back alley, where his bike was resting against a lamp-post, secured with a bike lock.

"Good evening, Ombudsman!" Giovanni cried. "Are we going for a night ride?"

"Open up, Lock," Gabriel said and made the Sign of the Covenant.

He put on the hood over his head and jumped on the bike. He dashed down a side street with a swarm of drones following him, a raggedy demon in a hat by his side.

"We're on the road again, Ombudsman," Maurice said. "Where are we headed?"

"I don't know yet," Gabriel said.

"Whatever you do, you have to be careful. This world is full of secrets," Maurice said, and his reddish-yellow eyes shone like molten lava.

Gabriel looked down the road to the city skyline glimmering

on the horizon, throwing a purple shade on the night sky above. The cool wind from the sea hit his face and pushed the hood off his head.

"Maybe I will find my father," Gabriel said.

And then, suddenly he saw an enormous face of a young woman, beautiful like a goddess, blue and transparent, spreading out above the lights of skyscrapers, and he understood that he was seeing the soul of the city for the first time, the soul of Los Maines, and she was staring into the mystery of the future with her cold eyes. She turned her head that covered half of the sky and set her eyes on him: a little teenager, riding his bicycle in an alley on a distant border of the city.

EPILOGUE

Meanwhile, that night, on the other end of Los Maines, his friend from school, Andrea, was asleep in her spacious bedroom in a suburban home.

Shadows moved along the walls and crept onto the ceiling. Andrea frowned and moaned in her sleep.

Once again, she was having the recurring dream of whispers among dark branches, and something talking to her, something inhuman that lived hidden in the leaves, in the grass, in the stream.

THE END OF BOOK 1

Made in United States
Orlando, FL
05 August 2024

49931316R10143